I0729346

LOVE LIKE A CEPHALOPOD

CASSONDRA WINDWALKER

2nd Edition
Copyright © 2023 by Cassondra Windwalker

All rights reserved.

No part of this book may be reproduced in any form or by an electronic or mechanical means, including information storage and retrieval systems, without written permission from the author, except for the use of brief quotations in a book review.

The novel is entirely a work of fiction. The names, characters, and incidents portrayed in it are the work of the author's imagination. Any resemblance to actual persons, living or dead, events or localities, is entirely coincidental.

Paperback ISBN: 978-1-7377525-8-5
E-book ISBN: 978-1-73777525-7-8

Printed in the United States by Bayou Wolf Press
Bayou Wolf Press
Mobile, Alabama
USA
www.bayouwolfpress.com

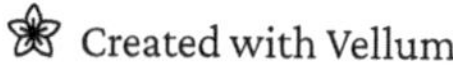 Created with Vellum

For my sister, Paula JoAnn,
to whom

many-tentacled love comes naturally

PRAISE FOR
CASSONDRA WINDWALKER

"I loved it! This dark novel has a plot with punch that also delivers clever and subtle layers of superb insight into human nature and society. I felt so much for Grenda's situation, understanding the lies she told herself to survive whilst absolutely willing her to change position and act! Perfect for readers who like their dystopian fantasy with a splash of political side-eye."

— MARIANNE HOLMES, AUTHOR OF *ALL YOUR
LITTLE LIES*

"*Love Like A Cephalopod* is a wonderful window into the people history forgets, those who are perhaps morally gray figures though integral to radical change all the same....."

"I love Cassondra's storytelling. Her writing just envelopes a person with soothing prose, even when depicting traumatic events."

— TIFFANY MEURET, AUTHOR OF *LITTLE BIRD*
AND *A FLOOD OF POSIES*

1

Her last words, I think, will always haunt me.

"You still don't understand anything about octopuses, do you?"

It rankled, how calm she sounded, even under these circumstances. The dragon on my wrist, sensing my irritation, drew back his vermilion lips to display the kittenish, needle-sharp teeth, and he huffed his leathern wings slightly. I laid a hand on his ridged back, and he settled down.

To this day, I don't believe Magenna was guilty of the charges. At least, not as they were stated. Witchcraft has always seemed a nebulous thing to me. Too easy an accusation to lob at anyone who speaks too often to ravens or owls, who lingers too long in moonlight, who possesses too rational an understanding of herbs and flowers and fungi. Even then, I wondered if the danger lay not in access to some mythical magick and more in the alternative it offered to the dictates of the state.

But if belief is a dangerous liability for an executioner, skepticism is even greater. True safety lies only in acceptance for acceptance's sake.

It doesn't do for a woman in my position to believe or disbelieve anything too strongly. The sentence must be carried out regardless, and beliefs sour quickly into guilt and regret. It's better to walk entirely in the grey and trust without exception to the system that hands down the verdict. Let them deal in black and white. My dragon and I, we were creatures of mist. We walked in fog, obscured from all but the walking dead. It was a peculiar irony, that the only people who saw us, who knew us face-to-face, were those who would shortly die at our hands.

I am only truly real here, chatelaine at the gateway to death.

And you, should I have ever met you here, would be more real in this moment with me than you had ever been in all your life. Contrary to how stories like to depict us, executioners aren't hard-hearted, unfeeling creatures. We can't be. It's not enough to kill the body, after all. We have to be sure to send the soul on its way, too. Malingering isn't good for anyone. And a soul simply can't go if it hasn't been seen. My dragon helped the dying shed their skin, and I – I helped them shed their invisibility.

That's all a ghost wants. They don't persist to wreak some paltry vengeance only the flesh-bound could imagine as a motivation. They don't need you to provide justice or peace. All your work is here, on this plane marked by hours and rot, and cannot reach them. They only need to be seen. Once. For who they are. Then they can go on.

So if I did my job right, the condemned were less likely than anyone to stick around. And I was very good at my job.

Some people – maybe even most people – are seen long before they meet death. But the people most likely to cross that bridge with my dragon and me rarely had been. If they'd been seen for who they were, they'd probably never have ended up here with us. It's not about innocence or guilt. It's about who sees you, as you are.

I didn't answer Magenna's question. She knew the answer already. I looked at her, and she looked at me.

Magenna's veins ran cold like currents deep in the ocean trenches, her heart fluttering faintly as it met mine. A little fear, only a very little. I wanted to take it from her, but I resisted the urge. She had very few things left to claim as her own, and this last fear was one of them. In her eyes, a hawk rested on a column of air, suspended dauntless above an endless chasm. And under her skin, the octopus stretched and unwound its long limbs, reaching for me.

My breath matched the rhythmic pulsing of the octopus' gills, and I felt the weight of the water rippling evenly along my body. I shifted as the sea-beast altered its colors and textures to match my own, and suddenly I was confused as to whether it looked like me, or I looked like it. The octopus' alien, slit-pupiled gaze had become Magenna's gaze, and I fell further in, seeing colors no woman could see, as if they were grains of sand sifted through my fingers rather than bands of light. A thousand soft mouths sucked at my body, pulling the skin, rearranging the bones into a shape that feared no pressure.

Then all at once, they let go. I was back in the cold, sterile room of death, with its harsh electric light and faint antiseptic smell. My subject lay slumped over her own arms on the table between us, her brown hair curtaining her face from any further trespass. My dragon kittered softly in my ear, his talons clutching my forearm, his dark liquid eyes fixed anxiously on my face. I saw the smear of blood on his white teeth and knew the task was done.

That was totally out of order. Dragons didn't act on their own volition. Bonded to their keepers from the hatch, they were nonetheless wicked clever, and one drop of their venom could fell an elephant within two seconds. Even a hint of rebellious tendencies resulted in immediate termination, a process that usually occurred within the first few days of their bonding. In the rare cases I'd read about where a dragon was terminated later in the relationship, the executioner invariably went mad.

None of that is exactly common knowledge, but little in an executioner's library is.

Nonetheless, I had no doubts about Bjartur. I understood that when the octopus had reached through my arms, tasting every inch of my intentions, it had directed Bjartur to complete the execution. I'd been wrong to think fear was Magenna's last possession. Volition, too, she held fast still. This un-wicked un-witch who lay silent and unbreathing on the table had staged one final insurrection, not submitting to her death but rushing to meet it as boldly as any beserker. Unnerved as I was, I could hardly fault her for it.

I rose to my feet, and Bjartur fluttered from my arm to my shoulder, tucking his emerald head well into my gray corkscrew curls. Time to deal with the ordinary people, those we'd neither execute nor see or engage any more than absolutely necessary. Bjartur wasn't shy – far from it. The unbonded were invariably fascinated by dragons. Bjartur didn't mind the attention, exactly. He just considered almost everyone else beneath his notice. He refused to be put on display or used as a symbol of anything for anyone. It's a common trait among dragons. They're notoriously catlike in their dignity and their arrogance. I can't explain how that makes them all the more irresistible, but it does. I adored the pretentious little puffer.

I pushed the button beside the door, and the guard on the other side keyed me out. Cleanup wasn't part of my responsibilities. The husk of the woman I left behind – her name had been Magenna, but the body needed no name – would be burned, its ashes scattered in the ebullient gardens that ringed the Justice Center. It's not as callous as it sounds. The part of her that was real was gone, after all.

Upstairs in my windowless office, I typed up the execution report on my typewriter and submitted it. Executioners don't have to muddle with tiresome machines like computers. Don't have to, aren't allowed to, what's the difference, really? Bjartur settled down between my shoulder blades, his talons resting on the harness there while he buried his head against my neck, under my hair, and snored softly, his sulfurous breath uncomfortably warm on my skin. I was well-used to it, though. That's another catlike feature of dragons – they are inordinately fond of naps.

Although executions have stepped up significantly in the past few years, it's still not a nine-to-five job. That's why in spite of the fact executioners possess more status than almost anyone outside of the president, my office resembled a broom closet more than an executive suite. Besides, windows were a security risk, especially here in the heart of the city. I spent a handful of hours there a month, so the grimness didn't trouble me.

Most of my actual work was done at home, well outside of city walls. As one of death's many gatekeepers, I kept the hinges swinging both ways. Ushering people out, and dragons in. A dragon clutch can take upwards of ten years before it's ready to hatch, and caring for them is a full-time job.

I was reaching for the door, on my way to the garage where my car waited for me, when it swung open and nearly smacked me in the face.

Naturally. My favorite person in the Justice Center.

"Fiske." I made no effort to imbue his name with the least enthusiasm. Our feelings were mutual and required no subterfuge.

"Grenda." He nodded, irritation at having been caught off-balance at the door flashing in his eyes. Fiske was a man of little talent and much presence, so he was easily perturbed.

"I'm on my way out, Fiske," I stated the obvious. "What do you need?"

On paper, Fiske would have appeared to be my boss, but that was only true in as much as he was the one who assigned the executions. As far as I was concerned, that made him more my assistant than my superior, and he knew it.

"It's going to be a busy week." He pulled himself up to his full height of over six feet tall, a futile effort to intimidate me. I'd hit my maximum height at the age of eleven and was barely five feet tall. Somebody's bones being longer than mine never impressed me much.

"Magenna Hassan was my only appointment this week."

Fiske bared his nicotine-yellowed teeth at me in what I can only assume he thought a patronizing smile. "The Army just notified me they successfully closed down an invaders' camp near the coast. It's going to be all hands on deck for at least four days. So be sure you're back here bright and early in the morning."

Something uncoiled in my belly, something that felt eerily like the slimy, seeking tentacle of an octopus. I swallowed the sour taste in my mouth and nodded briskly. Fiske's face contorted as he tried on a few different expressions, all intended as dismissal. I pushed past him without waiting to see which one he landed on. Laughter bubbled in my throat to watch him sway back until he nearly fell over in the effort to avoid any contact with Bjartur.

Silliness, of course. Dragons were perfectly safe. Or rather, my dragon was as safe as I was.

2

My driver dropped me off at the immense gate that kept the walls around my little home secure. He would have preferred to drive me up to the door, but I had little enough freedom as it was. I had no way of knowing how other executioners behaved, but I had long ago drawn what few lines I could between myself and the state that owned me.

He waited to ensure the guard at the gatehouse closed the iron securely behind me before pulling away, the expensive motor purring almost silently.

I didn't know my driver's name, wouldn't recognize his face if I saw him in a crowd. Dark, bulletproof glass kept us apart as we traveled, and we didn't speak. I caught a glimpse of him as he held my door for me, of course, but between his sunglasses and the frequency with which drivers changed assignments, looking for familiar features would have been a waste of time. And while I say *he*, genders likely changed as often as identities, but the standard uniform gave nothing away. The state had an interest in ensuring that drivers, like the guards posted on my property, developed no particular fondness nor favor for any executioner. We were too powerful, too feared, to be permitted the luxury of allies.

All of our luxuries, all of our indulgences, were only gilt chains.

My home would have seemed anticlimactic to any visitor who made it past the forbidding walls with their rolls of razor wire. Those grim reinforcements might have led one to anticipate some fiercely-defended concrete and steel monstrosity, but my little house was nearer to a fairytale cottage. Limestone walls, mullioned glass windows, window boxes overflowing with flowers, and a squat chimney added to the illusion. A winding flagstone path led to an intricately carved wooden front door.

Random scorch marks on the lawn did rather ruin the effect, thanks to Bjartur. Dragons are somewhat like mountain lions in that while their size is not impressive, they require a fair amount of territory. I didn't realize when my training began, all those decades ago, what a hidden blessing that would be. Had Bjartur only needed half an acre to thrive, that half-acre would have been the size of my entire world.

But dragons are sensitive, hothouse creatures, easily depressed. I've often wondered if the diminished potency in dragon venom when they're feeling low isn't some evolutionary failsafe, a way of ensuring the dragon won't be able to turn its little incisors on itself and put an end to its own existence. And it at least kept any captors from insisting on cruel practices that might have lowered the marvelous efficacy of the animals.

At any rate, the state needed dragons to be as deadly as possible, so my little abode stood on about a hundred acres of mostly forested hills. Bjartur could wander there at his leisure, though he preferred my company. At night, he hunted alone, stuffing his little round belly with crisped moths and fat cicadas. This suited me just fine. Those sticky-footed little fliers give me the heebie-jeebies.

That night, as we always did, Bjartur and I checked on our little clutch before doing anything else. Three precious eggs, their iridescent shells gleaming like opals, breathed quietly in a little wooden

manger carved of alderwood. A boot box would have done as well —
dragon eggs are only about the size of goose eggs. But I appreciated
the ritual worth of ornamentation. Besides, as a person entirely solitary but for my dragon, hobbies are requisite for maintaining sanity.

It's not so trite as you think. I wasn't some sad dealer of death
who needed the consolation of creation to find worth in her hours.
Even at my worst, I was only a conduit for the justice of the state.
Bjartur and I didn't condemn anyone. If you knew the history of
capital punishment in our country, you'd realize that we were the
hands of mercy.

All sorts of horrors predated the development of the executioner
system. Hangings, firing squads, electric chairs, ineffective poiso-
nous injections that left a subject writhing in agony for several
minutes before the body finally shut down. Sheer barbarism.

All those methods involved substantial security accommodations and costs. A single execution could take a decade or more to
carry out, depending on appeals, back in the day. This rendered the
whole system both ineffective as a deterrent and inhumane as a
practice. A man might remake himself entirely in a few years' time,
until the man put to death resembled the man who committed the
crime in name only. And with most of the public citizenry privately
as appalled by the sentence as by the misdeed, increasing the rate of
executions did nothing for the presumption of justice.

The discovery of the dragons changed everything. Docile to
whomever they imprinted, beloved and fascinating to everyone else,
and terrifying lethal, they provided the state exactly what it needed.
Dragons might not be the creatures of magic the old stories claimed,
but their existence nonetheless lent the state the seeming authority
of some higher power.

The painlessness and immediacy of death by dragon venom
silenced some of the concerns of detractors, and the dragons themselves silenced any others. In a nation burgeoning with overpopulation, illness, poverty, depression, climate change, and crime, peace
by dragon transformed the landscape. The National Council for

Advancement identified areas of concern and suggested new sentencing guidelines intended to curb overpopulation and pollution while enforcing civil norms and improving conditions for the people most likely to succeed.

The people Bjartur and I saw, the ones we escorted to their graves, were criminals whose actions either posed a significant risk to the community or to themselves. Most often it was the latter. It hardly made sense for any society to continue to spend time and money and precious resources on people whose choices repeatedly injured themselves and those around them. The depressed, the addicted, the generally self-destructive were purged as soon as they could be identified. They were usually happy to meet their end in a comfortable room, with an executioner willing to see them truly, fully, faithfully, as no one else in their life would do, at the mouth of a beautiful creature they'd only ever dreamed of meeting. And whether they admitted it or not, most of their family and friends were relieved that the waiting, the awful anticipation of that next phone call, was finally resolved.

Run-of-the-mill murderers, thieves, stock market marauders, gangbangers and their militia counterparts, met the same end without much contestation. Because by far the least common but still inescapable sentence was issued for enemies of the state itself. So-called witches like Magenna, philosophers and theologians alike who proposed any ethical guidelines but those of the state, seditious rabble-rousers, and of course, those who I'd be seeing out for the next few days: invaders.

I pushed the thought out of my mind. That'd be work enough for tomorrow. Tonight, I only wanted to listen to the quiet humming of the dragon eggs, eat my supper, work my jigsaw puzzle, and watch Bjartur fall off the edge of the table as he dozed, again and again.

It might seem strange that the dragon eggs were kept in the house rather than in some stable or barn, but most people don't understand dragons are highly social creatures. Honestly, it explains so much about those old tales of knights sallying forth against dragons. Even as a child, those stories were too fanciful for me. If dragons could fly and breathe fire, why would they even fight a knight? Why not just fly away?

If you understand that for centuries, dragons and people lived in the friendliest of company, the dark truth lurking under the fairy-tales becomes clearer. Humans are treacherous creatures in any period of history. When they decided to betray that friendship in order to rob the dragons of the resources of their dens, humans wrote those histories with noble men and immense, vicious vipers. In reality, stunned and traumatized by the brutality of people who had been their friends, the tiny dragons simply took to the air and left their lairs to the degradations of man.

The infant dragons sleeping in these eggs in my sitting room weren't that different from a human baby in its mother's womb. If I laid a warm hand on their shell, the baby dragon would shift and turn, pressing a knobby little head or as-yet-untaloned foot against my palm. They liked to be talked to, to be sung to, to generally be in company. The colors and songs of the eggs changed according to the moods and activities of the infant. When they slept, their colors dimmed to shades of violet and gray, and only the faintest of hums rose from the shells. When they were active, rainbow hues rippled ceaselessly over the surface, and all sorts of discordant melodies, still somehow pleasing in their strangeness, rose from the clutch.

They had to be kept warm, and they preferred the darkness. So a blazing fire on cold nights and small table lamps were my only illu-mination in this room. I'd draped their manger in a brown velvet canopy, to keep the sunlight at bay.

Bjartur accompanied me to the manger, laying his emerald head against the shells as if listening and fluffing up the straw around them with a delicate talon.

The gestation of dragons being so long, this was only my third clutch. The first time, I'd made the mistake of naming the little fellas, which made parting ways so much harder in the long run. Since then, I tried to think of them like blackberry bushes or wild grapevines, beautiful living things that immeasurably improved my life but existed to be eaten. Eventually, when the glowing shells became veined with gold, they'd be distributed to the executioners on whom they'd imprint. When new eggs became available, I'd make room for them, like digging out a fresh bed in the garden.

Bjartur sang over the eggs while I fixed my supper, his song a low rumble that evoked mountain thunderstorms or rolling breakers. The eggs added their much higher voices to his, and I felt complete contentment as I added cream and cheese to my soup. Later, while he hunted, I would read my ragged copy of *The Books of Earthsea* aloud from my rocking chair near the manger.

The evening passed without the slightest disturbance. As darkness fell and the day's heat slowly subsided, fireflies rose in glowing clouds above the meadow. The summer song of the southern wood joined the melody of the eggs. The wooden rockers creaked beneath me. Tea steamed from a forgotten cup.

I don't know why I dreamed about octopuses that night. With my eyes closed against the darkness, the sea itself streamed through my veins, and I drifted fearlessly with those mysterious aliens, tangled in their tentacles, attendant on their destination.

But when I woke, with Bjartur curled as always on my feet, disquiet rushed through me. It had been a long time – so very long – since I had tasted the sensation, but my tongue told me it was terror that trembled on my lips.

3

Executioners have no contact with one another or other dragons. I didn't even know how many of us there were. But based on my own schedule over the next several days, we were all feeling the strain.

The rate of modern executions far outpaces those of the past, but taken as individual events, the methodology of dragon and imprint takes much longer. An electric pulse or a rope or a needle don't take long at all. To actually see a fellow human being, to look into their soul and acknowledge them as a sacred soul, is a process that requires time.

It can't be rushed. Our country has long suffered the effects of unseen deaths. Ghosts of hidden genocides, public lynchings, the unsought-missing, the bodies piled up just past safety at the border, the hungry, the cold, the hated. No nation can survive that weight for long. Historians used to tell us that the cycle of power was inevitable, that it was only the socio-political evolution of ideologies, but now we know better. Kingdoms and nations fall when the weight of their misdeeds on the land grows too heavy. When blood seeps through the soil and poisons the crops. When the unseen dead outnumber the unseeing living.

I don't know for sure, but I suspect this is one reason why witchcraft is considered such a serious crime. Witches move too easily between the planes of existence. From what little I know, their so-called magic powers are nothing more than the ability to see what was and what has been, what persists and what withers. Where I could only see the living, they can see the dead who linger.

No state long tolerates any peer to their power.

Unsurprisingly, the invader camps often include quite a few witches when they're broken up. To undertake a journey of thousands of miles over either land or sea and cast all your possibilities into the unknown requires as much help as possible from both the natural and the spiritual worlds. After all, the invaders aren't armies. They don't have arsenals to back up their desperate maneuvers. They are only what we used to call refugees.

I didn't know how our political shift had affected the numbers of foreigners flocking to our shores, since none of that was public information in those days. We weren't the land of the free anymore, but we were the land of the safe. Our natural resources, which had always been immense on the world scale, now supplied a much smaller and more manageable population. We had some of the cleanest air and water in the world. Our crime rates were enviable by any measure, but especially when taken against those nations where cartels and political armies roamed at will. And it was still entirely possible to disappear into the wilderness of the interior. So it only made sense for many people to continue to risk everything to make it across our borders.

Bjartur and I were a significant deterrent, though. Where our country used to simply round people up and push them back across our little imaginary line, now invasion earned the captured an automatic death sentence. No trial was necessary. Just a quick trip from the border to the nearest executioner and their dragon.

I won't try to justify myself to you. My occupation was the cost of my own survival. We all do what we have to if we want to keep breathing. And it's not just myself I had to consider. If I died, Bjartur would most likely follow me. At least that's what I assumed. I didn't know for sure what happened to dragons if their executioner preceded them, but the Justice Center wasn't noted for its benevolence. Even if he didn't simply waste away, which was a definite possibility, he'd have been useless for their purposes, and our society was anything but tolerant of the useless.

I'm not sure why I explain this. There was nothing unkind in what Bjartur and I did. I've yet to meet a person who wasn't grateful to share their departure with us.

Even so, it was a long few days, and as always, we started with the youngest. It would have been cruel to make the infants and children wait, fearful, uncertain of what was happening, separated from their caregivers. And once the children were gone, their families were only too eager to join them. It was easiest for everyone this way.

Fiske was waiting for us in our office when we arrived, and I saw the fat sheaf of files he'd placed on my desk.

I walked in exactly on time, and I grinned cheerfully at him as he struggled between irritation at having been kept waiting on me and the desire to convince me he'd only just strolled in. He hated coming to my dank little cubicle, but he knew better than to issue me a summons to his corner office upstairs.

"You're going to be busy for a while, Grenda. I hope you ate a big breakfast."

"Your thoughtfulness is so appreciated, Fiske." He also hated that I wouldn't call him Mr. Fiske.

He snarled at me in what I'm sure he thought was a smile. "Might be a late night," he cautioned me.

Now that *was* out of order. I squinted at him balefully.

"I don't keep late nights, remember? I have eggs at home. You're just going to have to accommodate them for however long it takes."

Fiske flushed but to my surprise, stood his ground. "From the top, Grenda. Bare minimum is twenty-five a day for the next six days.

If we can, I'll let you take some time after that, but this shipment needs to move."

That gritty taste of fear that had coated my teeth when I woke up this morning rushed back into my mouth, and I coughed, trying not to choke. I'd heard from my trainers, back when I first started, of times like this back when the new state was just taking hold, but never in my three decades of service had I been asked to perform more than three or four executions a day.

I glared, hoping my consternation hadn't shown. Hostility is my usual go-to for uncertainty. In his harness between my shoulder blades, Bjartur shifted and thrust his snout around my neck. I had no doubt he was adding his baleful stare to my own. I tried not to wince as his little talons dug into my flesh through my blouse. He was well-used to my general dislike for Fiske, but he'd picked up on my much-higher-than-usual level of anxiety and was ready to come to my defense, if necessary. In spite of everything, I couldn't help taking a mean pleasure in watching Fiske's face blanch under Bjartur's gaze.

"You better warn your secretary to expect plenty of food orders from me, then. And be sure she just hangs them on the door this time. It's the height of unprofessionalism when an execution is interrupted by an order of extra-crispy wings and loaded fries."

Fiske nodded and began edging out of the cramped room. "Of course. You know we are here to support you in whatever you need."

His tone might have been perfunctory, but the statement was factually true. Fiske's title outranked mine in the sense that it carried more weight in polite circles, whereas mine evoked dread fascination, but he and his entire staff were basically my handlers. Fiske didn't even determine who was scheduled for execution. He only passed on the message.

As soon as he left, I picked up the phone and dialed Shovel's extension. I was sure she had a name. It seemed everyone did. But if I despised Fiske, I loathed his secretary. And since she had a face like a shovel, that was what I privately called her. So far I hadn't said it out loud.

She spat out her usual static when she picked up the line, like she didn't know it was me and not some random outside call.

"I guess you've heard it's going to be a long day," I told her. "How about we start off with an order of tamales? And be sure to get plenty of the green sauce. And napkins."

Her exasperated sigh was all the food I needed, really. Shovel much preferred me to order delivery, so she only had to march her clackety heels down two floors to me after she'd accepted the delivery. My own interaction with the outside world was limited as much as possible. My knowledge of this preference of hers was almost the entire reason I ordered tamales at least once a week.

My office didn't have a window, but the execution room did. It really was the loveliest room. It had the same impact on everyone who stepped inside it, which was probably one reason Congress had been so willing to accept its existence. The walls were stucco and a pale, sage green, lined here and there with bookshelves. With actual books, even. Buttery soft, overstuffed leather chairs practically begged to envelop you. The windows were draped with pale gold sheers that lent the whole room a dreamy light. Nubbly blankets draped across the furniture as if your grandmother had just left the room. The table and my own chair were constructed of deeply stained carved wood.

It was from that window I had first seen the tamale lady. I'd had to ask one of the guys from upstairs what she was doing, trucking up and down the busy city street with her hand cart. He explained she made tamales in her kitchen at home, and after she'd completed her deliveries to her regular customers, she set up shop on the sidewalk till the rest were gone. Then she went home. Maybe at ten in the morning. Maybe at four in the afternoon. Some days she didn't show up at all.

I have a hard time explaining why she appealed to me so much. From what little I saw in my narrow-windowed perspective, she lived entirely on her own terms. She decided how many tamales she would make. She showed up when she wanted and went home when she wanted. She made friends of strangers who loved her first for her skill with cornmeal – how strange a connection is that – and then for who she was. The suit I'd asked about her had fairly lit up as he explained her business to me.

To create such adoration in someone simply by feeding them appealed to me. I wanted to be one of her customers. I wanted to be one of her friends. I wanted to know which day she always made the kind I liked best and rush down to the street to meet her before anyone else could buy them. I wanted her to keep aside a little of the sauce she knew I liked best and to share anecdotes with me about the stuffy banker on the corner and the guitar player on the square.

That was nonsense, of course. I couldn't do any of that. I wasn't even allowed out on the street.

So I consoled myself by making Shovel chase her down. I knew it offended her pink suit sensibilities to be high-heeling it down the sidewalk to beg for a sweating plastic bag redolent of peppers and oil from a dark-skinned woman whose whole home might have been the size of my broom closet office. Sometimes, if I wasn't with someone, I would watch from the window as Shovel gave the tamale lady my order. I'd pretend the tamale lady knew they were for me, pretend she would squint up at me and nod her head in a quiet acknowledgment of our kinship.

She never did, of course. But she was far enough away that I could pretend.

Bjartur perked up when he heard me mention jalapeno sauce. Happily he never competed for my tamales, but he did love the green stuff. I'd never admit to Shovel that it's way too hot for me. I only demanded it for Bjartur's sake. Well, that, and the satisfaction of knowing Shovel had to engage with the tamale lady that much longer to secure my precious sauce.

I left the files on my desk. I'd only need them when it came time to file the reports. As far as the executions went, I just took them as they came. Very few things written on paper are relevant as far as the soul is concerned. My task, remember, was to see the person for who they are. Not everything they've ever done or been accused of or all the nasty checkboxes life has lined up against them.

The actual person.

Which as often as not bears very little resemblance to those deeds, be they awful or not. Oh, sure, there are plenty of terrible, cold people out there. But most of them are quite successful in society. The ones I meet?

Generally the sort of people you'd really like.

Just kidding. I have no idea what sort of people you'd really like. I've never shared a pint or played pool in a bar, never commiserated at a parent-teacher conference or homeowners' association meeting, never chatted with a stranger in a bookstore.

Never talked to a tamale lady.

Even so, I'm sure you'd have liked my first execution that day.

Bjartur and I were standing at the window, sharing our mutual amusement at Shovel as she wandered uncertainly down the sidewalk, hunting the tamale lady, when the escort came in.

Escorts were like guards or chauffeurs. They changed too often and were too distantly professional for me to distinguish one from another. Their task was simply to lead my subjects into the room and leave them with me.

I almost saw this one. Startled by his burden, I looked into his dark eyes and as quickly looked away, hurt and somehow blunted by the tears I saw gleaming there.

My subject hadn't walked in, shackled and bound. She'd been carried.

Carried. In a tiny, pale yellow blanket.

I know I already explained the rationale behind why infants and children were eliminated first and how humane that solution was. But right up until this moment, that rationale was purely scholastic. I'd never terminated an entire invader camp myself.

I'd never executed an infant.

It's mysterious even to me, but my hands didn't shake as I took the precious bundle from his? – her? – arms. I'd gone cold, all the way down to my belly. All the way down to my toes. Even Bjartur, on my shoulder, shivered as if he felt the chill.

The baby looked up at me in perfect trust. Impossibly long lashes fluttered up against her mono-lidded eyes. Her tiny eyebrows were mere whispers of color, a hint of an idea she'd fill in when she got older. Her weight reminded me of Bjartur when he was sleeping, a warm, heavy fullness that felt like peace cradled against my belly.

The escort made an indiscernible noise and stumbled backward out the door, closing it behind them with what would have been a bang had the hinges allowed it.

I sank into one of the leather chairs, clutched the baby to me, and looked deep into those blue, blue eyes.

4

Swimming into her was as easy as stepping from light into darkness on a cold winter night. Infants have no defenses, no painfully constructed walls of consciousness. One moment I was in my own skin, and the next moment I was in hers.

Language drifted like paper snowflakes, their edges flared and cut with clumsy scissors, never quite sticking to anything. She had a mother, but like most invaders, she was a child of many arms, many blankets. She was not afraid to pass from one embrace to another, because all embraces were warm, all embraces were comfort, all embraces were safety. Even the gray curls dangling above her face were familiar, and she reached for them, holding my hair tight in her tiny fist as she drew me nearer.

I wanted it to take longer. I wanted it to take forever. I wanted to hold this little sweating bundle of possibility and perfect faith against my chest, to feel her powerful thudding heart against my own, wanted to lose myself in her blue eyes that looked and looked and looked and saw everything. I wanted to relearn the shapes of life, to have never been told how things are and instead trace out for myself their edges. I wanted to cry without shame and laugh without compunction till my belly jiggled. I wanted to find the universe in the shape of my toes.

But the sad truth is that the execution of a baby takes no time at all.

Bjartur climbed splay-toed down my arm when I pulled back into myself. The baby's eyes widened in awe, and she dropped my hair to reach for him. He placed one scaled foot in her palm, ever so gently. He couldn't retract his claws, but he curled them in against his own skin. Her fat fingers squeezed him tightly with the spasmodic uncontrol of the very young. So very quickly, his needle-teeth pierced the flawless skin.

Her fingers unwound from his glittering claw. Her gaze, still fixed on him, lost its fascination and glazed over, blue lost in a mist that did not dream. It suddenly seemed a terrible poverty that I'd never heard her voice. She hadn't cried, hadn't gurgled or giggled in the scant moments I'd held her.

She was still warm, still heavy against me, but her heft was now somehow boneless, its animus fled. Bjartur curled around my neck, feeling my ache in his own bones. She wouldn't have wanted to live as an orphan, used by the state until her expediency was exhausted, I lied to myself desperately.

It was too late for lies, though. I'd already seen her. Not as she was defined by the Council, but as she was. She had wanted to feel Bjartur's scales under her palm. She had wanted to look into his multi-lensed eyes. She had wanted to be held. She had wanted to talk to him in her baby-babble and see if he would talk back to her.

But Bjartur and I, we had stolen all her want away.

I hit the buzzer, passing the still bundle back to the escort who waited there. I took a brief and merciless refuge in my office, a space that offered silence but no consolation. Bjartur, still looped around my neck, hummed low in his throat, a quiet sound of self-soothing that signaled his own discomfort with our task.

I pulled down the top file as I sank into my chair. Shovel wasn't Ms. Personality, but she was efficient at least. The files were without exception in perfect order. From my left, the oil-heated fragrance of chiles rose from the bag of tamales. Beside the bag stood two large, perspiring bottles of water, one for me and one for Bjartur. I guzzled mine greedily, feeling as though my guts were going to be a desert for the rest of my life. I pulled Bjartur's bowl from a drawer and filled it with water, too. The dragon reluctantly unwound and tiptoed down my arm to the desk and relieved his own thirst.

Infant Invader, the file read. I wondered bitterly how old a person had to be before they were given a name, before they were considered an independent sentient being. I was suddenly, horribly sure I was going to find out in the course of this day. Numbly I rolled my report template into the typewriter's feed, and my fingers flew, automatically completing the fields with the pitifully few details required.

I pulled out another dish and dumped the jalapeno sauce in it, adding a few dried crickets from my stash. Bjartur's eyes sparked at that, and he happily slurped up the lot. Normally Bjartur had eaten enough from his hunting the previous night to last him through the day and only snacked as an act of indulgence. Today, though, was going to test us both, and no doubt he'd need all the sustenance I could find for him. Personally, I had no appetite at all. Even breathing felt superfluous now.

I rang up Shovel. "Miller moths," I told her succinctly. "To my office, please."

I could have flipped through the file folders, found out how many more infants and children I would have to execute today, but if I'd done that I could never have left the room. Sometimes it's better to face things only as you must, if you're ever going to get through them at all.

I stood. Bjartur froofed his leathern wings, circled the room a couple of times, then landed on my shoulder. He shuffled sideways to slide down into his harness and laid his head against the back of mine. Even on this grimmest of days, he felt like peace.

Four. There were four more infants. I realized, eventually, that they must have split up the youngest executions among the dragons, so that no one of us had to do them all. Perhaps they knew how much this was to ask, how nearly they might drive us to an edge from which we could not retreat. Even as someone who'd never been around a baby before, someone who had always known she would never carry a child of her own, there was a particular horror in executing an infant. It's not as though executioners aren't empathetic people. Quite the opposite. We have to be empathetic, if we are going to bond with a dragon, if we are going to be able to see people well enough to grant them the peace they need to leave this plane behind.

And while the mind continually tries to shut down, to block out the awfulness, to redirect the attention to anything else, that doesn't work when you have to proceed from one execution to the next like an assembly line worker. I was wholly engaged, up to the very tip-top of my soul in the act of humaning as truly, as deeply, as gently, as I could. There was no way out. There was no way through. There only was.

It came as a terrible shock, then, to understand that executing an infant wouldn't be the worst thing I'd be asked to do that day. Toddlers were far worse.

I have executed children before. In some ways, children are the easiest to escort from one world to the next. Bjartur has a gift for befriending even the most doubtful of them. And while many adults are too jaded to even want to believe anything good, children are the opposite – they may dread an outcome, but if you give them a reason to believe in something good, they will. I tell the truth: I am a gate-keeper. All I do is open the gate. And they, when they feel ready, walk through. Into a world whose magic is different than ours, but more enchanted, not less.

I haven't been asked to execute many children. I suppose, if I gave you the number, it would seem like a lot to you, but it's a matter of ratios. Compared to the adults I've helped cross over, children have accounted for a very few. And invariably, the children brought to me are badly broken. This world has betrayed them. Abused them. Tormented them. Abandoned them. They need a better place to go.

But when an escort walked into the execution room holding the hand of a little boy who might have been two or three, my heart seized up so badly I thought I might actually die. Bjartur curled around my arm like a serpent ring and keened softly under his breath.

The child was dark – dark skin, dark hair, dark eyes that pooled with murky tears. He sucked his thumb, dragging his feet. He possessed none of the trust of the infants, none of the comprehension and curiosity of an older child. He was all fear and loss and dread.

I dropped to my knees, hoping to ease his anxiety. I stretched out my arm (an impressive feat, because Bjartur is much heavier than he looks,) thinking the dragon might coax him nearer. But he dropped his thumb and howled with terror, clawing his hand free of the escort and running for the door.

I glanced up and caught a glimpse of the escort as he turned to retrieve the boy. The first escort, the one whose soul I'd nearly opened, the one with tears in his eyes as he'd brought me that first baby, hadn't been back. This man's face was impassive, with only a hint of weary exasperation behind his eyes. As if this moment were no more affecting than recapturing an escaped chicken and returning its head to the chopping block.

Surely, I thought, my mind reaching for any mundane detail to which it might cling rather than the bleak reality before me, *surely this boy has a name on his file.*

No detail of that moment, however mundane, could offer a reprieve, though. It was awful, wretched, ugly, up to the very end.

The escort pushed the boy toward me and exited swiftly, the door closing behind him with the same unhurried sweep as always. The boy backed up against it, his wide eyes fixed unmoving on Bjartur.

At my silent urging, Bjartur retreated to his harness. His bony chin rested on my shoulder, and I knew only his snout and sparkling eyes were still visible under my hair. He huffed, a hot little snort of air signaling his discomfort. I lowered myself the rest of the way down to the carpet, crossing my legs and resting my hands on my knees.

"My name is Grenda," I said softly. "I'm sorry my friend scared you. His name is Bjartur. Have you ever seen a dragon before?"

The boy shook his head slowly in response to my words, but I saw no comprehension in his eyes. The odds were very good he didn't speak English.

"Bjartur won't hurt you," I said. The words made my heart hurt. They were true enough, in their way. The boy's death would be painless, but it would still be death, and what deeper injury was there than that? "He's curious about you. What is your name?"

He rattled something in the garbled tongue of the very young, and I wasn't sure I could have understood him even if he were speaking my language.

"It's good to meet you," I continued, hoping the tenor of my voice would soothe him somehow. Anticipating my next request, Bjartur clambered down my chest and curled up in my lap, butting his bony skull against my palm as I petted his scaly skin. The boy's head cocked, and he dropped to his knees, crawling closer by slow degrees.

Bjartur hummed an off-key melody. The boy smiled, ever so faintly, and hummed back.

Within a few minutes, the boy's legs were crossed in mirror of my own, and one small hand tremulously stroked the ridges on Bjartur's back. His fear was fast fading into wonder as he bent closer to peer into one of Bjartur's kaleidoscope eyes. Bjartur blinked his long lashes at the boy's approach, and the boy unexpectedly burst into giggles. My heart clenched. I might not understand his words, but delight and joy speak universally.

This is why I'm here, I told myself fiercely. *To make this moment one of grace and beauty instead of agony and terror.* True as they were, the words tasted like cardboard on my tongue.

Playfully the boy scooted his face closer to Bjartur's, and again his laughter pealed as Bjartur rose to the occasion, frantically fluttering his lashes. The boy looked up at me, all trepidation fled, inviting me to join in his mirth.

I did, of course. It's who I am.

No time left.

My gaze seized his, and I dropped into his soul like a salmon dropping down a waterfall, heading for the sea. I felt him as he slipped his hand into mine, and ever so gently, I rotated his arm, baring his wrist for Bjartur.

Soul-seeing is an experience out of time. I doubt it was even two seconds before Bjartur's flashing jaws sent that sturdy little boy body tumbling across my lap. But oh. The life I saw.

Mama and Papa. The roiling sea. Spinning stars, hanging so low he could nearly seize them in his fist. Puppy fur and slobbering kisses, left behind. The taste of honey. The smell of warm bodies and safety, pressed against him in the darkness. The fantastic mathematical poetry in which his mind took everything apart and put it back together.

He'd have been a scientist, maybe. An engineer. An inventor. A father who knew just how to fix the car, build the shelves, put Humpty Dumpty back together again.

And now he was gone, a heap without hope where he'd been laughing a moment ago.

I resisted the urge, new and strange and awful, to pull him into my arms, to look into the slack face and will him back to life. He had been seen, his place emptied, and now he moved on paths I could not see.

Gently I moved the body, at once so heavy and then not heavy enough, from my lap to the carpet. Bjartur scrambled into his harness as I stood. I'd only completed five executions so far, and it was already ten in the morning. Funny how death can take so little time while life continues to race past.

Seeing. Executing. Writing the report. Watching Bjartur dart and dive with glee as he chased handfuls of miller moths around the cramped space. Cramming something I couldn't taste into my gullet. Tormenting Shovel out of mindless habit. Doing it again. And again. And again.

By the time mid-afternoon rolled around, I felt like a piece of fine-grit sandpaper. I wasn't the flesh, raw and bleeding. I was the abrader. And still, I had to reach inside myself, find the place that breathed and believed and wept, and open it to the next soul whose vehicle I would steal. That place became all that was left inside of me. All the other hallways and rooms and balconies of my own soul were bare.

Then I met Allora.

5

Allora's face gave no hint of what lay within her. She was probably eight or nine years old, and she'd learned to hold fast the integrity of her body. When the escort pushed her forward and left, she stood with her heels pressed together in a pair of shapeless sweatpants, her hands clasping her elbows. Her chin was up, her lips pressed tightly together, and her eyes glittered with the most beautiful rage.

I couldn't help returning that fury with a smile. There is something precious and clean in unabashed, unapologetic anger. She was the oldest child I'd seen yet today. Bjartur's hum almost lilted into a warbling song as he picked up the frequency of her ire. She was so very painfully alive.

When her eyes fell on Bjartur, something shifted in her, and her body fell open. She dropped her arms and stepped forward, fury vanishing in fascination. Bjartur stunned me by racing headlong down my body and crossing the carpet to twine himself around her ankles, his song increasing. She squatted down and stroked his sinuous body without a hint of fear. The dragon butted his head against her legs and practically grinned.

"Come sit," I said, gesturing to one of the overstuffed leather chairs. Only about half of the children spoke a little English so far. She understood my meaning at least and complied readily, laughing as Bjartur continued to wrap himself around her steps, threatening to send her sprawling. When she sat down, Bjartur climbed up her sweatpants and installed himself on the arm of the chair, looking for all the world like a little gargoyle on duty.

Uneasiness I'd never felt before prickled through my limbs as I stood under the dragon's glittering stare. According to the old stories, if he was the gargoyle, that made me the evil spirit, didn't it?

I rolled my shoulders, shook my head. What a silly idea. Bjartur and I were bonded, had been since the day he left his shell. He would never place himself in opposition to me. He was just a dragon, perched on the edge of a chair next to a little girl. And I was just suffering from an overactive imagination.

I should be glad the child's fear had been so easily assuaged, I told myself. I might as well get this over with as quickly as possible. The day had been long and horrible enough already without prolonging the inevitable. So I sat in the chair beside her. Automatically she mirrored my posture, turning so that her eyes met mine, and I saw her.

Only I didn't see her. I saw Bjartur, his two hearts beating slow and steady, his multifaceted gaze ignoring me and remaining fixed on the girl. *Friend*, the word a rusty, laborious effort, drifted up through his mind. Bjartur preferred to communicate without the handicap of speech, but he was quite gifted in language. He thrust the word at me, forcefully.

I leapt up from the chair and stumbled backward, pointing at the girl like a histrionic villain in a Victorian novel. Nothing like this had ever happened before. I wasn't sure it was happening now. I struggled to frame a question from the impossibility I was sensing.

"You," I said weakly. "You – you can see Bjartur. You can talk to Bjartur?"

She scowled in confusion and drew the dragon into an embrace, wrapping one skinny arm around his body and petting his head with the other. At first I thought she didn't understand me, but then she spoke.

"I talk to dragons. You talk to dragons. Same."

Horror and confusion suffused me. It wasn't just that she was able to join her mind to Bjartur's so seamlessly that when I looked into her, I only saw him. It was that she possessed defenses of her own that kept me from seeing her.

She was right.

Same.

She was like me.

I looked helplessly at Bjartur as if he would advise me, but he only lifted his upper lip in the faintest snarl of warning. That had never happened before either. I understood what he meant, though. We weren't going to execute Allora.

I sank back into the cushions, my mind racing. I suddenly realized I didn't know as much about dragons as I thought I did. I'd always assumed my relationship with Bjartur was entirely intimate, that our connection only existed between the two of us. I thought each executioner and dragon were uniquely paired.

But maybe it was much simpler than that. Maybe just like I could see into – almost – anyone and encounter their true soul, dragons could connect with any human who possessed the same gift. I peered anxiously in Bjartur's direction. Maybe he didn't love me as much as I thought. Maybe I was the only person he had to talk to and he'd been making do all these years. My stomach clenched at the thought.

A dragon snort in the back of my mind reassured me that Bjartur wasn't inclined to make do with anything. Nonetheless, his defense of Allora was implacable. She, for her part, clutched the dragon closer and raised her chin at me.

I liked her, but then, I liked most people. It is impossible to see a person for all that they are and not love them at least a little bit. Even the ones deeply stained with evil have a place inside them the darkness hasn't reached, a place that merits genuine pity if nothing else.

I buzzed the escort. "Get Fiske," I told him when he opened the door. He gawked at me and opened his mouth to protest, but I closed the door. I never wasted time explaining myself to those people, and I wasn't about to start now.

You're probably thinking my social skills leave something to be desired, and maybe you'd be right if I lived in the same world as everyone else. But I didn't. I didn't have friends. I didn't have coworkers – at least, not any that I knew. I had Fiske and Shovel and those other interchangeable automatons who did as I asked. They were not allowed to engage with me, and I'm fairly certain they were too scared of me and Bjartur to want to. I've heard of the internet and how these computers talk to each other across the air, but it's as real to me as calculus. Meaning, not very. I have something like a phone in my house, but it only rings to and from the Justice Center. My parents both died when I was ten.

That – my mind shies away from the memory. That was devastating.

After that, a cycle of tutors and caretakers moved through our home. My parents must have been very well-off, whatever they did, because there was never any question of me having to leave. It was very hard in the early days, as I couldn't seem to help forming attachments to the people cycling through my life, but they never stayed long. Not only that, but there seemed to be no rhyme or reason to their tenures. Sometimes six weeks, sometimes eight, sometimes two. There was never any warning, never a goodbye. One day they'd be there, teaching me math or cooking supper or mowing the lawn, and the next day someone else would be in their place. Eventually I learned to hold myself apart.

I didn't learn that on my own, though. Like spelling or literature or geography, my gift for seeing came with its own lessons. I was taught how to find the true self, buried under all the stories that had been told to it, all the stories it told itself. How to divide the spirit from the language or languages that limited and muzzled it. How to keep my own walls staunchly up, although that came more naturally. Even a dog hides its belly till it trusts you. And I was also taught how not to see, how to move blind among people and bear up under what would have otherwise been a ceaseless onslaught of spirits starving to be seen.

That is part of the reason the loss of my parents affected me so deeply. Our relationship was like mine with Bjartur: no boundaries, no barriers. Just love and comprehension. To lose that so suddenly was like losing all my limbs and being told I had to climb a cliff-face to survive. Impossible.

But I did survive. And I did learn to live without any connections at all, until I met Bjartur. So now I didn't waste my time on petting and stroking the sensibilities of people who were as real to me as paper dolls. The only people who mattered to me were the ones we killed.

It was gratifying how quickly Fiske appeared, since I knew how much he'd have loved to make me wait but daren't risk it. As the door closed behind him, his eyes darted nervously from me to the girl with the dragon in her lap. She seemed to realize that this man was not a friend to her, as she set her mouth and cast him one of those baleful stares I was becoming so fond of.

"What – what's happening?" he asked.

"You tell me. This one - " I waved in her direction, since I hadn't yet seen her file and didn't know her name, "can't be executed."

To my surprise, immediate comprehension bloomed in Fiske's eyes—comprehension which baffled and enraged me. Why did he know what this meant, and I didn't?

"Ah." He rubbed his hands briskly together. "She'll come with me, then."

Then he frowned. "She's quite old, though, isn't she? Not sure what we're going to do about that."

"About what?" I demanded. For once Fiske didn't seem intimidated by me. He was thoroughly distracted by the new problem I'd presented him.

I preferred him intimidated.

"Nothing for you to worry about," he told me grandly. "Get up, little girl. What's her name? And get your dragon back." That last bit was directed at me. Rather rudely.

He knew I didn't read the files beforehand. I think he liked forcing me to admit ignorance to him, not something that often occurred. "I don't know her name. Why don't you take Bjartur away from her yourself?"

Fiske narrowed his eyes at me. I laughed.

"Fine," I conceded, though inwardly I had my own doubts. Bjartur had left no question that he wouldn't execute the girl who still clutched him to her chest, and I wasn't at all sure that he'd allow her to leave with Fiske. But at my silent summons, he opened his wings, pushing the child's arms aside, and flopped gracelessly through the air to settle on my shoulder. It wasn't easy to fly in such a small space. Still, I suspected that his talons yanking my hair as he settled into his harness were deliberate.

All the same, I felt oddly reassured he'd acquiesced so quickly. He must have known Fiske posed no immediate threat to her, or I was sure he wouldn't have complied at all. Why it suddenly mattered so much to me what happened to her would have been hard to explain, except that she was the nearest thing to a – a what? A friend? A relative? A peer? that I'd encountered in more than forty years.

It was like being stranded alone on an alien planet for decades and suddenly finding another human being.

I knew better than to give Fiske any inkling of my feelings, though. I kept my face as disinterested as I could. "There's no other executioner around here," I asserted baldly, although I had no way of knowing if that were true or not. I watched his face closely.

Damn it. He was watching me just as closely. This was the very rare occasion that he had the advantage over me, and he had no intention of surrendering it.

"I'm well aware of our resources," he said, reminding me, unnecessarily, that I was a commodity of the state, not a citizen. Executioners and their dragons came out for parades and major state events where plenty of cameras were present, but otherwise we were totally divorced from civic life.

"Come, child." He gestured to her again. Her broad-featured face, not dissimilar to my own, grew even haughtier in suspicion, but she slowly rose and walked toward him. I had the distinct impression she did so only to save herself the indignity of being dragged. Very queenly, this bedraggled little invader imp. I liked her even more.

I followed them out, only to save myself the inconvenience of having to buzz the escort again. I knew better than to try and follow Fiske wherever he was headed with his ward. I tried to part ways without a backward glance where the hallways diverged, but I couldn't resist sneaking a look after all. The girl had pulled her hand free of Fiske and walked stiffly beside him, more like a little queen with her escort than a doomed child.

As soon as we were safely ensconced in my office, Bjartur clambered around, his talons clutching my shirt (there's a reason I don't favor silk blouses) and stuck his snout in my face.

"What did you want me to do?" I groused, grabbing the next file in the pile and flipping it open. "You know Fiske wasn't going to just give her to us like some kind of stray puppy."

There was her photograph. A sullenly defiant young girl in the colors of a muddy desert river at dusk. Myself, I was canyon cliffs in moonlight. I often wished humans had the palette of dragons – greens and purples, scarlet and gold, but we are all the color of dirt and sand. It made sense for us to be like the earth where we were bound, while dragons reflect stars from the skies they so easily master.

Her file, as always contained precious little information: Her nation of origin, the location where she was detained (and by which agency and officers), her age. I'd guessed well: she was eight years old. Her last name was Ishil, wherever that was from.

Bjartur nipped impatiently at my chin. I was unfazed. Dragons release their venom consciously, and I knew Bjartur would never hurt me. But he had no qualms about pestering me.

"Liked her, didn't you?" I soothed him absently. "But she's gone now. It's not like I can get her back. You're just going to have to make do with me."

Bjartur huffed. I plopped into my chair and dialed Shovel's extension.

"Sushi," I told her shortly. "The usual order. Also, I need you to get me an octopus for the house."

I waited for her squawking to subside.

"No, not to eat. To keep. Like a pet. Have the tank installed in my bedroom. And be sure the installers close my bedroom door when they leave the house."

I hung up the phone with her still in mid-sentence. Any protests she wanted to make were for show, and we both knew it. Bjartur and I might live on something of a deserted island, but at least it was a luxury island. I had little doubt that she'd manage to acquire everything necessary to keep an octopus alive and have my new roommate waiting for me by the time I got home.

The rest of the afternoon passed much more slowly than it should have. I didn't know if Allora had really been the last of the children, or if Fiske had done some last-minute shuffling to ensure that the rest of the week would be adults, but at any rate no more children visited me. I should have been able to process the adults quickly, but I was struggling to put Allora out of my mind.

Any one of the adults I saw that day could have been her parent, her aunt, her uncle, her grandparent. Every soul spoke to me of fear, of bereavement, of becoming, but I had no way of knowing which of them, or if all of them, were connected to the mysterious girl. I wasn't a mind-reader, after all. I don't doubt there are telepaths out there. I've often wondered if in fact Bjartur is a true telepath, forever frustrated by my stunted mind. But I'm just a seer. I don't read a person's thoughts. For me, language is a barrier. Words only limit the way you frame yourself. I look past language and see the self, indivisible.

Nobody said Allora's name to me. She could have belonged to any or all of them. Maybe she'd been orphaned before they'd ever begun the journey to our country. Allora's file said she'd come from Cuba, but that might have only been her most recent stop. Where she'd been before then was anyone's guess.

My mind kept wandering, trying to fit together a puzzle for which I had only one piece. No, two pieces. Allora and me. Somehow, we were alike. It had been so long since I'd felt a kinship with anyone but Bjartur, and the moment had been so brief. I didn't want it to be over yet.

More weirdly still, I felt an odd responsibility for the girl. I told myself she was no doubt already dead. If I hadn't encountered anyone like her in thirty years, there probably weren't enough of them for the Council to worry too much about the weight their ghosts would leave on the land if they died unseen. Likely Fiske had just taken her down to the nurse's office and had them administer a lethal dose of something or other.

I couldn't convince myself she was gone, though. So after I'd finally completed my last job for the night, I marched myself up to Fiske's corner office.

He wasn't happy to see me, but he didn't look surprised, either. He motioned Bjartur and me to a chair.

"What'd you do with her?" I asked without preamble. "What *was* she?"

Fiske sighed, taking off his glasses and cleaning them as if that would buy him time. "She's not your problem anymore, Grenda. You deal with the dying. Leave the living to me."

I felt Bjartur perk up and tried to keep glee out of my own eyes.

"So she's not to be executed, after all? Was there some kind of mistake?"

"The Council doesn't make mistakes, Grenda, you know that. But there's only one way to know what she is – what people like her are – and that's to meet someone like you. Now that we know, we'll deal with her."

"What'd you mean, she's too old?"

Fiske shook his head. "You don't need to know anything about her. Put her out of your mind. You'll never see her again. We all have work to do to keep our country safe. You do your part, and I'll do mine. That's all there is to it."

I sucked my lips between my teeth. Fiske's voice had an unusual undercurrent of steel. Keeping his eyes carefully away from the dragon on my shoulder, he placed his hands on his desk and stood. "Go home," he told me. "Get some rest. You have a long week ahead of you still."

Reluctant to say anything that might sound like surrender, I held my tongue and left the room. The drive home passed in a blur. I closed my eyes and leaned against the leather seats, comforted by the warm rumble of the dragon curled on my lap.

At least I would have an octopus waiting for me at home.

6

The night before, when I woke bug-eyed from ocean dreams, I'd switched on my bedside lamp and trotted over to the row of encyclopedias on the bottom shelf of the book-shelves that made up three of my four walls. I ran my finger across their spines till I reached one labeled *Menage/Ottawa.*

There were only four paragraphs on octopus. Intelligent, secretive, solitary. Finding one small enough for a bedroom tank wouldn't be a problem. The only issue would be keeping it occupied. A bored octopus was an escaped octopus, as often as not. And dragon eggs might not be their preferred diet, but I didn't doubt they'd be willing to try something new, given the chance.

Why would I even contemplate such a risk?

I wasn't sure myself. Magenna had infected me somehow. Perhaps I was mistaken about witchcraft, and there was more to it than I'd credited. Maybe her last act had not been to take control of her own death but to enchant me, to curse me with some obsession that would be my undoing.

I didn't believe that, though I chuckled at the thought. I did think she understood something I had missed, and I was hungry for that knowledge. In my world, a world I knew was small by anyone else's standards, knowledge was everything. My only hoard.

I was a voracious reader. Often I read aloud to Bjartur, who would let me rest my book on his belly as he lay purring on my lap, his four taloned feet splayed in the most ridiculous position. Over the years I'd collected an immense number of books. I'd give a list of authors to Shovel, and she'd have their complete works delivered to the house.

My appetite was too great for my space, so I only kept the books I knew I'd want to read again and again. The others I devoured and then placed in the wooden box on the back porch. One day it would be full, the next it would be empty. I didn't know what they did with the used books – donated them, perhaps, to libraries or schools.

I was aware my understanding of contemporary society was limited. Everything I knew was only what I read, and much of what I read had been written before the Restructuring. I wasn't troubled by this, though. What difference did it make to me how other people lived, what the mechanics of their grocery shopping or dinner parties or math tests looked like? I knew who people were. I carried with me the echo of every person whose soul I'd seen. And I had Bjartur. I was anything but lonely, and I didn't need a connection to the constructs of commerce to understand my purpose.

I did love to lose myself in other worlds, though. Fiction or nonfiction, I devoured them equally. Astronomy and poetry, botany and romance, Mobius strips and the Fibonacci sequence – I could never tire of exploration, and I didn't need the comfort of a city street or a train car to believe that I was going somewhere.

But aside from the odd reference to the Kraken or other sea monsters, I hadn't given much thought to octopuses before Magenna, and somehow, she'd known that. Known it, and thought it accounted for something absent, something lacking in me.

I'm aware that the few people, like Fiske, who know me, find me cold. Maybe they're right. Only the dead can testify to the warmth of my heart. Maybe a cold-blooded octopus, dwelling in shadows, black ink and canny subterfuge its only defenses, can teach me something about myself. Maybe I am more akin to them than to any warm-blooded biped stranded on land.

Probably not. But I wanted to find out. And there was no reason not to indulge my curiosity. I was confident I could keep the beastie contained and occupied and well away from my precious eggs.

As always, the house was immaculately clean when I came home, its pantry stocked. Once upon a time, live-in housekeepers who cooked my meals cycled through the house with the same irregular regularity as my drivers, but not long after my eighteenth birthday, I'd sent them away, and to my surprise, they'd gone without protest from my keepers. At that moment, I learned that inside the gates, my power was nearly supreme. I'd grown to resent the intrusion of strangers who didn't care for me, about whom I'd never be allowed to care myself, and dispensing with them had been a rush. A heady, exhilarating rebellion against the system dictating my existence. Now my little domain belonged only to Bjartur and me and the crea-tures who inhabited the woods and the hills. An empty caretaker's cottage stood behind my house, beside the gardener's shed. I knew they came when I was away, but they crossed my mind less often than the furniture these days. I only thought of them when I left a list of grocery items I wanted delivered or some new seeds or bulbs I wanted to plant.

My octopus would have to wait. Forcing my anticipation aside was one more exercise of will, one more proof I was more than the pampered slave they thought me. I went straight to my eggs, turning them gently. The warmth emanating from their marbled shells grounded my spirit, filling me with peace sorely needed after the executions of the week. Bjartur crept around them like an anxious grandfather, laying his cheek on their curves and burbling softly to them. Once he'd satisfied himself as to their comfort, he wrapped himself around them, his barbed tail gently undulating along their rounded edges as he closed his eyes, content. These long days were hard on him, too.

Throat tightening with excitement, I opened my bedroom and slipped inside, closing the door again right behind me. I was not disappointed. Shovel might have the personality of a mannequin, but she was a highly efficient mannequin.

Rows of book spines magnified weirdly through the huge tank set up directly opposite my bed. Large rocks formed dens and cubbies and plants of indeterminate color waved gently in the water. I dropped to my knees and peered closely. Finally I spotted a small tentacle resting on one of the rocks, the remainder of the creature's body obscured in shadow.

"Hello there," I murmured. I didn't think the octopus could hear me through the glass and the heavy-duty lid preventing its escape, but not greeting my new roommate was an impossibility. "I wonder what your name is."

Unlike dolphins or seals or whales or the other animals of the sea with high intelligence, octopuses don't use language, but they do have a sense of self. What was it like, I wondered, to think without words? To recognize and imitate colors without having a name for them? Was that an innate function of being a rational creature devoid of relationships, who continually perceived and deconstructed reality but had no one with whom to share or argue the concepts?

"How about Morrigan?" I asked her. I couldn't be sure this octopus was female, but I decided I could forgive myself this small projection. "Seems appropriately powerful and mysterious."

In the corner nearer my bed was a much smaller tank containing several crabs. Octopus food. This tank had thoughtfully been placed out of sight of the octopus, so at least Morrigan's days wouldn't be spent in frustrated attempts to reach them.

Or perhaps, successful attempts. Based on my limited reading, octopuses were accomplished escape artists.

I rushed back to the living room, anxious to introduce Bjartur, but he was snoring softly by now. I decided to cook supper instead and host their meeting later, before he rose to conduct his nightly hunt. I raised the windows, although the warm summer air was little cooler than the house. Still, the breezes tossing the curtains and the cicada-song rising from the woods lifted my spirits. As darkness fell, the night would cool further so that I didn't sweat beneath the sheets. A warming pad under the eggs kept them regulated. I could always turn on the air conditioner, but I put off its rattling, canned intrusion as long as I could, preferring even sultry winds to the chill that only came with shut windows and shut doors.

I don't remember what I ate that night. Again and again, my thoughts returned to Allora. Where had Fiske taken her? What would become of her? If she was like me, did that make her useful enough to live? I left Bjartur and my eggs to their somnolent singing and dragged a chair in front of the tank in my bedroom, chewing absently and watching that one tentacle as my mind churned.

Clearly Fiske would be no help. Whatever the truth was, he didn't want me to know it. I wondered if the answers might be in Shovel's filing cabinet or - I swallowed hard – on her computer.

My computer skills were pitiful. Even my reports were prepared on what I knew was considered antiquated equipment by everyone else. I'd picked up the most basic understanding of what the machines could do while looking over other people's shoulders as they typed away, but that was the extent of my knowledge. Most of the time I was standing on the opposite side of the screen. I'd never even been much interested before; as far as I was concerned, they'd only represented more menial tasks I didn't have to do.

Now I wished I knew something, anything, about the virtual world that seemed to dictate the lives of so many. I was suddenly keenly aware of my disability. I'd thought it freedom: freedom from false constructs and pretend worlds, freedom from endless screen tasks that blinded the user to reality, freedom from constant noise and static. But that night, I felt trapped, blindfolded, my ears stuffed with cotton, while all around me strangers saw and spoke and moved, unhindered. And somewhere in that room where my percep-tion was chained was Allora, if only I could reach her.

The summer sun had still been up when I came home, but now it was all but gone, long shadows stretching across my bedroom floor. I let the darkness settle comfortably over my shoulders like a cloak, my eyes adjusting to outlines cast by the dim purple light emanating from the octopus tank.

Morrigan emerged.

She was unspeakably graceful, her tentacles seeming to drift effortlessly on invisible currents, her billowy head resting on a pillow of water, when in fact thousands of micro-movements bent the water to her will. She was very small, only a few inches across, and I hoped she would not find her tank too confining. I sat motionless as she explored her habitat, her tiny suckers tasting every centimeter of plant and rock.

Finally I slid from my chair and pressed a palm to the glass. She darted away, back behind the outcropping of rocks where she had lain when I came home. I waited. Ever so slowly, she eased back out, her skin seeming to ripple as she adopted the colors of the pebble floor beneath her. Even with my eyes locked on her, she all but disappeared as she crept nearer. Finally one tentacle floated upward like a scrap of seaweed till her suckers reached the glass between my extremity and hers. She clung there a long while, no doubt frustrated by the disconnect between vision and sensation. I held my breath, transfixed by her tiny, slit-eyed gaze. Strange that so minute a difference between us – the shape of a pupil – could render us so very foreign to each other. All the other differences – the scaffolding of our guts and muscles, the texture of our skin, the mechanics of our breathing, the construct of our skies – could be overcome with mankind's relentless anthropomorphizing of all we encounter, but Morrigan's stare somehow made us strangers.

I jerked nearly out of my skin when Bjartur's scraping talon on my bedroom door broke the silence, and Morrigan pulsed away in a blur of bubbles and black ink. I rocked back on my heels, laughing a little at myself as I tried to slow the gallop of my heart.

"I'm coming, you damned cat-dragon."

Bjartur hopped across the floor when I opened my bedroom door. He was unaccustomed to a closed door when we were at home and no doubt had been thoroughly irritated when he woke from his nap to find me behind one. I'd learned when he was just a baby that separation was poorly tolerated. Even when I took my baths, I had to crank up the heat in the little room and leave the door open, or he'd torment me the whole time, scratching at the wood and stretching his arms as far under the door as they'd go. With the door open, he usually pretended to be completely bored with whatever I was doing in there, content to leave me in peace after nothing more than a stroll along the edge of the tub. More than once he'd miscalculated the slipperiness of the sudsy porcelain and wound up in the water with me.

Believe me, a soggy, disgruntled dragon leaves quite the mark on bare skin.

His curiosity now thoroughly piqued, Bjartur flapped to the lid of the aquarium and leaned over, peering into the water much as I had done. Morrigan was well out of sight now; even that one tentacle hidden behind the rocks. I saw sudden tension ripple along Bjartur's shoulders and down his wings. Somehow, he sensed the other creature lurking in the shadows. Perhaps if I was right about Bjartur being telepathic, he and Morrigan could connect on a level I couldn't. At any rate, the dragon clearly knew we were not alone in my room.

"Her name's Morrigan," I told him. "She's an octopus. A friend from very far away."

I always assumed Bjartur understood every word I said. Maybe that was wishful thinking on my part, but I didn't think so. Dragons are very vocal creatures. Their own language, from what we've observed of those left to their own devices in the wild, has so far proven beyond our ken. Likely they found our crude tongue incredibly simple to decipher. Bjartur never seemed at a loss for understanding. And when he chose, he was perfectly adept at pushing words into my consciousness. Most of the time, though, they were unnecessary.

"She's shy," I explained. "She doesn't know us yet. We'll give her some time to get used to us. Are you ready for your hunt?"

For answer, Bjartur hopped on my arm and climbed up to my shoulder. I stood easily, long-accustomed to his extra weight. We generally began his nightly hunt together, walking across the gentle slope of the meadow to the verge of the woods. There I would let him fly on alone, his incredibly acute vision allowing him to sail under tree limbs and through brush as easily as any owl. Some nights I would see the smaller silhouettes of bats flitting around him as he dipped and soared, darting after the mosquitoes that were too small a prey for Bjartur. I wondered if the bats felt a companionship with the dragon, or if he represented some protection from the raptors who likewise hunted through the twilight and the dark.

Tonight's evening sky held no imprint of the day's horrors. Deepening violet stretched into gloaming blue, with only the sheerest hint of tangerine on the horizon bearing witness to the sun's passage. Southern air holds onto the heat as long as it can, so the night was scarcely cooler than the day had been. Perhaps in the wee hours, temperatures would drop. Dragonflies still dashed and hummed through the long grass, unwilling yet to cede the night.

I felt Bjatur's talons grip as his muscles bunched and he pushed off, his powerful little wings swimming through the sky. I heard untroubled rustling just past the edge of the trees and knew the deer wandered there. We were all well-accustomed to one another in this place. The fear and dread I inspired in those outside my gates did not follow me here. Here, I was only another animal, secure in her place.

Unhurriedly I returned to the house, the low glow of light through my windows no challenge to the stars who, one by one, broke through the darkness. I smiled, happy to think dragon eggs and an octopus were waiting for me, even if they didn't yet know what *me* was. Out there, beyond my walls, only grave-waiters looked for me, but here, I was a mistress of beginnings.

7

ear was so unfamiliar a visitor, he looked exactly like excitement.

I'd thought this morning was like any other, but when Bjartur and I slid into the backseat of our car the next morning, a note waited for us on the leather.

Don't speak, it read. *Don't attract the attention of the gatekeeper. I'm a friend. Someone needs your help.*

My eyes swept up. For a scant second, I met the obsidian stare of a stranger in the rearview mirror. Then his eyes returned to the road, and the car drove quietly away from my home, seemingly as it always did.

Had he left the note? He had to have done, but nothing in his demeanor gave it away. I kept reading.

You will be contacted at the Justice Center. Many lives depend on your discretion.

Slowly I folded the paper, over and over, and acting on some hitherto unawakened instinct, tucked it into my ankle boot. I looked at Bjartur, who gazed back at me unblinking, nothing more than a quiet tension in the posture of his wings betraying his awareness of our strange new circumstance. I turned my head to look out the window, my mind spinning with questions.

My life had been predictable and untroubled for decades. Sometime in my youth, I had adopted, or rather, been trained to a stillness of the soul I understood was peculiar to the people of my craft. I read extensively, so of course I understood the trauma and upheaval and uncertainty which typified most lives, but my reaction was more fascinated curiosity than empathy. All my trauma, my upheaval, had struck very young, and then, quite suddenly, my whitewater river subsided into a pool that scarcely permitted a ripple across its surface.

I had no doubt this aspect of my nature was identical among executioners. To stand witness to so many departing spirits, to accept and welcome the imprinted existences of people and dragons, required a reserve of quietude, a deep well of peace into which soul after soul could sink. Maintaining such a well came at a cost ordinary citizens could not imagine paying.

I did not know what it felt like to pay bills, to save pennies for food, to be cold in winter or hot in summer. I had no obligations outside of my duties to the Justice Center and to the dragons, but I had no liberty either. I didn't have to clip coupons, but I wasn't allowed to buy groceries. I couldn't drive. I couldn't walk outside my gates. I carried the weight of the dead, but I had no friends besides Bjartur. I never had to share anything with anyone, but then, I was denied even the small gift of a name, to know what any of the people who controlled my daily existence were called. Gatekeepers, patrols, housekeepers, drivers – I would always be surrounded by strangers.

All these truths created an invariable certainty in my days that kept my mind steady and untroubled. Bombs could have leveled every city in the country, and it would not have affected me unless a driver or a housekeeper failed to show up.

So the idea that this sudden conspiracy could have no connection with Allora was an impossibility. My life was devoid of novelty. Two unexpected events in two days' time had to be related.

Rebellion against the state was not even a consideration. I myself was the surety against such a reality. I knew the implacability of the response. Our nation hadn't achieved the cleanest air and water and lowest crime rates in the world by listening patiently to the excuses and appeals of those who defied state mandates and order. Step out of line, and judgment was summary.

So the fear thrilling along my veins and sending the hairs on my arm to attention was unfamiliar and unexpected. I had nothing to fear, after all, if I were faithful and loyal to the state.

And I was.

Wasn't I?

I knew what I should do. As soon as I arrived at the Justice Center, I would walk straight to Fiske's office, straight past Shovel's disapproving stare, and hand him the sweaty little note burning a hole in my shoe. No doubt later today, or tomorrow at the latest, the man sitting in the car in front of me now would be sitting in my execution room, surrendering his soul to be seen one more time before it left his body behind. Whatever accomplices he had would meet the same fate.

I wouldn't know, when they came to my room, who they were. I doubted I would even recognize the driver himself without his dark glasses and uniform.

He would probably tell me. Perhaps even beg for his life, as so many did. Once I took their hands, though, and stepped into the space of their spirit, they quieted. It was such a rare gift, to be seen. I had never yet known anyone to squander that moment, to sully it with vapid pleadings and pointless protestations.

Unwillingly my mind returned to Magenna. In all these years, she was the first to push back against my intrusion. That wasn't the right term for what she'd done, but I still wasn't even sure myself exactly what had happened. Somehow she'd taken the control out of my hands. Somehow she'd used our link to reach through me to

Bjartur and direct her own death. I still didn't know how that was possible.

Could she have been like me? Like Allora, but with the training and discipline to hide her abilities from me at first glance? But if that was the case, how had I seen her at all? Allora, after all, was identifiable specifically because she was beyond me. And Magenna was far from the only witch I'd ever executed. They were actually rather common subjects for me. But perhaps the range of the human spirit was greater than even I recognized. Perhaps all sorts of souls I'd never encountered still milled about out there.

I was so caught up in my musings, I was startled when I realized we'd arrived at the Justice Center. The driver opened my door, walking me to the private carpark entrance, where he handed me off to another guard and the x-ray machine that ensured no one smuggled weapons inside. Cold terror suffused me as I walked through automatically, and I stumbled, wondering if a small white square on my ankle would trigger a body search.

Things would move very fast. The search, the find. The restraints. The cell. The execution.

Stupid, stupid, stupid. I should have eaten it. Next time I would eat it.

Next time? my anxious brain screeched at me.

But no alarm sounded. The bored uniform glanced at the screen and flicked her eyes at me as she always did. Respectful, but sliding away. Uncomfortable. Afraid.

Bjartur fluttered over the machine and regained his spot in the harness that hung between my shoulder blades. I stiffened my trembling knees and strode forward as if this were any other day.

I didn't take the elevator to Fiske's office. I went straight to my own little broom closet, where Shovel had a hot caramel macchiato steaming on my desk. Shaking, I sank into my chair, pulled out the note, and dropped it into the hot liquid. It had to go down easier soggy with sugar.

I avoided Bjartur's penetrating stare as I stirred the weird concoction and gulped it down. The words I swallowed scraped my belly on the way down. *Many lives depend on your discretion.* Such an odd appeal to make to someone whose days were spent dispatching lives. Or so it had to appear to anyone on the outside. Somehow, whoever had penned these words knew that every life did matter. Every life was precious. I was not contemptuous of life: I was one of its many curators.

Without exception, the few people I saw every day responded to me with one of two emotions: fear or contempt. Sometimes both. What sort of person could possibly be appealing to sympathy on my part? Who could imagine that I would risk everything while knowing nothing of what they wanted, on this thinnest of entreaties?

Who could know that it would work?

Hastily I swallowed the dregs of my coffee. A stack of manila file folders, the day's executions, stared blankly at me from the edge of my desk. Another uncommonly long day. I yanked open my desk drawers, pawing through their few contents, but no hidden missive lurked there. I walked around the narrow room, peering in vents, checking underneath my chair.

Nothing.

Relief trembled on the edge of my consciousness. Maybe whatever the plot was had already been foiled. In a few days, a few weeks, the strange events of the past days would be an all-but-forgotten anomaly, a scant ripple already swallowed by stillness. I could return to the quiet rhythm of my hours, vouchsafing souls, walking with Bjartur, talking with Morrigan, turning the eggs.

That was it, then, I told myself. No need to think on it further.

As I walked down the hall to the execution room, Bjartur kneading my shoulders softly with his little talons, my head throbbed.

Ten executions before lunch. The pace was brutal for both of us. When Bjartur and I finally retreated to the office for a break, we buried our snouts in our food without so much as an exchanged glance – Bjartur in a bowl of red curry, and me in a platter of crab rangoons and sweet-and-sour chicken. The inside of my skin ached, and my eyeballs burned with over-sensitization. I could tell from the careful, creaky way Bjartur moved that he wasn't feeling much better.

This afternoon, I resolved, before I left, I would tell Fiske he was going to have to slow things down. Bjartur and I weren't machines. There was a limit to how much we could take. He would just have to figure out a way to spread things out.

When the last drop of curry disappeared down his gullet, Bjartur slid down onto his belly, legs akimbo, and closed his eyes. I wasn't sleepy myself; if anything, I was painfully wired. I scooped up our trash and called Shovel, putting in an order for maple doughnuts and chocolate eclairs. Bjartur had an uncommon weakness for crème, and I had no doubt we would both need an infusion of sugar in a couple of hours. She crackled her usual irritated assent.

I was unprepared for Fiske's recalcitrance when I told him Bjartur and I needed to reduce the daily rate.

"Can't be done," he told me brusquely, though he assiduously avoided my angry stare. "Everyone is all-hands-on-deck with this one. It's one of the biggest busts we've ever made. You're not the only one having to stretch herself here."

"Why not at least give us a few more days to complete them?" I argued. "A couple more nights in confinement can't possibly make a difference." I held out my arm, and Bjartur left his harness to walk down into my embrace. I held him against my chest, rubbing his forehead ridge as he growled happily low in his throat. Fiske shifted, clearly using all his willpower not to push his seat back to put more space between himself and the dragon.

I wasn't above a little intimidation, especially when it came to Fiske.

But for once, it didn't work. Fiske shook his head firmly. "These people pose a serious threat to national security. The Council is adamant these executions be carried out without delay. You and – and your dragon will just have to buckle down."

Easy for him to say, who had never borne a single psychic toll on behalf of another human being, much less two dozen in a day. I sighed, and Bjartur huffed angrily. A sheaf of papers on the edge of Fiske's desk rustled with the dragon's breath, and I grinned in spite of myself to see the brown singing their corners. Fiske grabbed at them and yanked them out of reach.

"Bedelia has pulled the week's files together for you. You can take them home and get a head start that way. She's already taken them down to your car for you."

I opened my mouth to protest that wasn't helpful in the slightest and then snapped it shut again. I loathed engaging with Fiske any more than absolutely necessary on a good day, and this was not a good day.

Also – *Bedelia?* Had I heard him call Shovel by that name before? If I had, it hadn't registered, not once in the ten years or more she'd been working for him. It sounded weirdly romantic, like a heavy-headed flower in a Victorian garden. I honestly couldn't conceive of a less romantic person. Her parents really missed the mark with that one.

"Fine," I conceded waspishly. "But you get to tell her tomorrow morning that I took her peanut butter cups."

I sailed out of the room and stalked to Shovel's desk – she must have already left for the day – and yanked open the bottom right drawer where I knew she kept her candy stash. I grabbed both the half-empty bag and the unopened one. I unwrapped a chocolate confection and tossed it into the air. Bjartur snapped it up with ease.

I could positively feel Fiske shaking his head behind me. Shovel would be even more delightful in the morning, no doubt. I had to take my compensation where I could.

Despite my irritation, I'd nearly forgotten what Fiske had said by the time the car pulled up to the gates at home. Bjartur and I roused from our dozes when the driver opened our door. It wasn't until I saw him walk to the rear of the vehicle and pop the trunk that I remembered Shovel's pointless chore.

On my shoulder, Bjartur stiffened, then relaxed into a tuneless song like those he sang to the eggs at night.

The driver yanked up a heavy file case on wheels and dropped it on the drive. "Would you like me to take it up to the house for you?" he asked.

His voice jarred. It's funny how you can honestly forget that people have tongues when they never speak.

"No, thanks," I responded, jealous of my poor privacy as always. *Great.* I took the handle from him. It'd be fun to lug this stupid thing back and forth for no reason at all. The wheels rumbled over the flagstone drive as the gatekeeper let us in. I half-suspected Shovel had loaded the damn thing with bricks just for fun. I seriously considered leaving it on the front porch, but with my luck, a summer thunderstorm would blow by and soak it through. The last thing I needed was some minor paperwork catastrophe that would add yet more hours to my schedule.

I propped the thing by the front door and tossed my stolen candy onto the coffee table, kicking off my shoes with a sigh. No way was I cooking tonight. Crackers and cheese and a cherry limeade would have to suffice. And peanut butter cups, obviously.

I was reaching for the jar of maraschino cherries when Bjartur all but barked for my attention. His rambling song had been getting louder and louder, but I hadn't paid much attention, assuming he was pandering to our little clutch. Now his voice rose insistently, sharply, and I turned to see what had agitated him.

He was perched on top of Shovel's ridiculous case, tugging anxiously at its locked zipper with a single talon. Apprehension bubbled in my stomach.

"What is it, Bjartur?" I asked, crossing the floor in two long strides.

I snatched my keyring off its hook and flipped to the tiny zipper key. I could count on one hand the number of times I'd needed to use the thing, and I'd been plenty irritated when Shovel insisted I carry the thing around. House key, the key to her filing cabinet, and the key to this rolling file case. My fingers fumbled as I unfastened the padlock and pulled down the zipper.

A small brown hand pushed the case open. I shrieked, stumbling backward even as I clamped a hand over my mouth.

Allora's dark eyes gazed steadily up at me.

8

The traitorous little winged demon on my shoulder abandoned me without a moment's hesitation. Bjartur fluttered to the ground in front of the child, who unfolded herself rather painfully from her confines. The dragon rubbed against her ragged sweatpants. The unfamiliar odors of child-sweat and fear wafted from the otherwise empty case. The girl's hair was plastered to her head. The anger I'd so admired had been replaced by anxiety. And probably terror.

Well, that was weirdly reassuring. I'd have wondered at the humanity of any child who could be trapped in what was basically a suitcase for at least an hour and a half, bumped around in the hot trunk of a car, and maintain equanimity. My brain scrambled fruitlessly to comprehend what stood in front of it; giving up at last, it seized on something simple.

"I'll get you a glass of water," I said.

When I came back, she was standing under the velvet canopy where the clutch lay humming. Bjartur stood perched on the edge of their little manger, wings spread, looking for all the world as if he were showing them off. I scowled at him. He ignored me.

"Don't touch them," I said sharply. "Here."

Noisily she gulped down the entire glass. I was tempted to immediately bring her another, but I decided to take it slow. I didn't want her hurling on the floor. I'd never been scrunched into a box in the trunk of a hot car myself, but I didn't imagine it did wonders for the digestive system.

"Hey! What'd I just say?"

She'd laid a hand gently along the edge of the shell nearest her, bending her head as if she were trying to make out more of the eggs' strange song. She cut her eyes at me, snatching her hand back. She might not understand every word, but my tone clearly got through to her. Bjartur huffed imperiously at me, tinging the air with faintest blue fire.

I rolled my eyes at him. Sure, she was being careful, but so what? No one but Bjartur and me had laid a hand on our little clutch since they'd been delivered eight years ago. Presumptuous little twit.

Still, I had enough of my wits about me to recognize that if Bjartur didn't consider the stowaway a threat, she wasn't one. As defensive as I was of our dragon eggs, I had nothing on Bjartur. In their natural states, male and female dragons are equally communal, and they all share the duties of caring for their young. With such a long gestation, and the earth being the dangerous place it is, it wasn't uncommon for one or both parents to be dead before the eggs hatched. So it was necessary for all dragons in the colony to adopt and care for all young as their own. Bjartur, however long divorced from his origins, was no exception to this.

Slowly, her obstinate gaze still fixed on me, she slid her hand back to one of the iridescent eggs. I shrugged.

"Fine, fine. What do I know? I'm just the dragon-keeper. Ignore me." I stomped back to the kitchen, where I sliced the blocks of cheese with more force than strictly necessary and shook out a box of crackers onto a platter. I smacked them down onto the coffee table and sank onto the leather couch.

"Come on, then. Eat something. I know you're hungry."

That got her attention. She abandoned the clutch and threw herself cross-legged onto the floor in front of the table, stuffing food into her face with abandon. She couldn't have missed that many meals, I mused critically. Prisoners were fed, after all. Even if she'd been hidden away the moment she'd left the execution room, that only accounted for about six missed meals. Apparently that felt like imminent starvation to a child.

Not that I knew what starvation felt like. But I didn't imagine invaders were accustomed to regular meals.

Okay. Time to back away from the immediate and figure out what was going on here. I might not know much, but I knew enough to face a firing squad, that much was sure.

Not something I'd ever given thought to before I'd encountered Allora, but clearly death by dragon was not an option for wayward executioners. I couldn't imagine any dragon being willing to sink their fangs into my skin, as Bjartur had demonstrated with Allora. So my end would no doubt be significantly less pleasant than what a dragon could afford me. Not to mention I had a feeling the Justice Center took it personally when one of their own executioners turned on them.

It wasn't an eventuality I'd even considered before. I was not enjoying the broadening of my horizons tonight.

"Who put you in that - " I waved at the still-gaping file case – "in that box?"

Allora answered me around a mouthful of smoked Gouda. "A woman. A woman like a rock."

Shovel, obviously. After all, Fiske had said she'd put the files together for me. But how could that be? Shovel was the least likely invader collaborator I could imagine. Could some other equally flint-faced woman have accessed the file case after Shovel had filled them with files and swapped them out with Allora?

The logistics were just too difficult. It would have been all but impossible for even Shovel, with all her access, to pull this off. For someone else to come along behind her, having a key not just to the file case but also to the trunk of the car, someone who could get in and out without attracting the attention of the driver or the carpark guards, was highly unlikely.

More unlikely than the thought of Shovel as rebel?

I chewed my own hunk of Gouda consideringly.

It had to be Shovel. It had to be.

Who else would know I had the key to the case at my home? I stood abruptly and walked over to the case, probing it with my fingers. Tiny holes had been poked all over its surface, invisible but to the questing eye, no doubt in hopes enough oxygen would leach through to keep the child alive. I thought of the sweltering Georgian heat, the close confines of the car trunk. Even with the holes, quite the risk. The child could have hyperventilated, died of heat stroke. Panicked and given away her hiding place at any moment.

Yeah. That sounded like a risk Shovel would be willing to take. She'd never struck me as the bleeding-heart type, to put it mildly.

If I were honest, though, it wasn't that disparate from a risk I'd be willing to take myself. At some point, you have to take the leap and leave everyone to their own devices. You can't want them to live more than they want to.

I shook my head. I did *not* like feeling any kinship with that bureaucratic creature.

Kinship. This whole situation was madness. I pushed myself back to my feet, sending the file case spinning onto the floor.

"Stay here," I said sternly to Allora, casting a speaking look in Bjartur's direction. The faithless beastie had better keep an eye on her.

I went to my bedroom and closed the door quietly behind me.

Somnolent violet light waterfalled down my walls, casting an unlikely pall of peace over the space. How could I have forgotten Morrigan? The arrow's flight of light across her tank as my door opened and closed sent her poofing hastily back behind her rocks. I took three crabs from the tank by my bed and dropped them under the lid of her habitat, taking care to fasten the lock back in place. The last thing I needed now was an escaped octopus on top of everything else.

She wouldn't eat them all right away - she was just a tiny thing. But I figured she could do with the anticipation, the challenge, the promise of prey. Predators crave the prospect of a good hunt.

I should know.

Already, it seemed, Morrigan was losing her fear of me. Mere seconds after the bubbles had stilled, she came creeping out—strange, graceful alien I so wanted to call friend. I watched her wrap her sinuous arms around a crab in the most fearsome of embraces. I knew from my reading that she was injecting a paralyzing toxin through the crab's shell with her one barbed tooth. Once she'd thoroughly incapacitated her prey, the shucking and feasting could begin.

I sat on the floor in front of her tank, cross-legged like Allora had been in the living room. Morrigan's attention didn't visibly shift in any way, but I felt certain she remained as aware of me as always. I wondered what her existence had been before she came here. I imagined a small tank in a large room, stacked among other sea creatures readied for sale. Did she still remember the ocean? Did she hope one day to find her way back, or did she merely accept whatever walls she found built around her?

I glanced around at my bedroom. My tank was bigger than Morrigan's, I thought. Or was it?

I banished the fatuous notion. I had more pressing matters to consider than some imaginary prison. I was freer than anyone I knew. Free from hunger, anxiety, cold, heat, or care.

Or I had been, until now. Now I had my own imminent execution sitting in the living room with wide brown eyes. Before I could decide what to do next, I needed some understanding of what had already happened.

For whatever reason, someone had identified me as a likely sympathizer with this hopeless cause. What on earth made them imagine a nearly sixty-year-old executioner who had spent her entire life in unflagging service to the state would suddenly throw over her life for the sake of strangers was beyond me.

The only other possibility, though, was that this whole escapade was an elaborate loyalty test. That seemed even more implausible. And unnecessary. I'd never given Fiske or any other boss the slightest reason to doubt either my devotion or my efficacy. Which brought me back to this mysterious cadre of fools who'd cast their lot in with my non-existent affinity for revolutionaries.

Shovel had to be one of them. Same for my driver this morning. Had he also been my driver this afternoon? Doubtful, but possible. Who else?

Someone had spirited Allora away after Fiske had disposed of her in whatever fashion he'd intended. But who? That was another question for which I had no answer. Had he meant some other purpose for her, or had he simply tried to execute her by some other means? Whichever it had been, at least one and possibly more people to whom he'd entrusted the task had betrayed him and helped Shovel abscond with her instead.

It struck me that the state must be in a more precarious position than I would have ever guessed, to have so many conspirators in a single Justice Center. Could the whole nation be a rotten loaf of bread, mold only just beginning to bloom on the crust but already spread through the whole? What did I really know of the state of society?

Nearly nothing, I concluded with a shrug. It had never mattered much to me before. My days turned on the same fulcrum regardless of the tragedies and triumphs of the strangers who filled the streets. I saw them as we drove through town, but from my distant perspective, they seemed as sentient as cogs. Some people walked this way down the sidewalk, some walked that. Some days they were all in hats and scarves, some days they all wore slickers or carried umbrellas, some days their flashing bare arms and legs glittered from crosswalk to crosswalk. Lights blinked and changed, wheels turned, screens summoned. None of it touched my life at all.

Suddenly my life had shattered, and I had no idea, staring down at the jagged pieces, what sort of mosaic I could possibly make of them.

The obvious answer was to walk out to the gatekeeper's post and tell them to contact Fiske, that Allora was in my living room and conspirators were afoot in the Justice Center.

I pushed myself to my feet. Morrigan, still holding fast to her dinner, scooted hastily back behind her rocks. I opened my bedroom door and rested my hands on my hips. Allora was curled on my couch, sound asleep, with Bjartur draped across her exposed side. The dragon lifted one lid, his untroubled stare making plain his expectation of my decision.

I sighed, turning on my heel and heading into the kitchen. Absently I mixed up two more limeades, dropping three maraschino cherries in each frosty glass. Of all things to be stingy with in life, cherries had to be last. Allora could probably use a little sugar in her system when she woke up anyway. I still couldn't believe she'd held herself still and silent in the cramped darkness and uncertainty and heat for as long as she had. What sort of straits had she already endured, on her journey to our shores, that made such self-control possible in a child so young?

I put her glass in the refrigerator and returned to the living room, flopping down unceremoniously in my leather rocking chair and glaring balefully at my charges as I sipped my drink. By some ridiculous and unanticipated coincidence, I'd managed to increase my responsibilities significantly in a matter of hours. I'd gone from tending a small clutch of dragon eggs with the help of my sole companion to playing mother to an octopus and an orphan.

When I thought about it, we were all orphans in this house. I was the only mother Bjartur had ever known. My clutch, like those previous, had been stolen away from their mother as soon as they were born. Morrigan's mother would have died of starvation shortly after her baby octopuses hatched. And my own parents were long dead.

If Allora's parents had made it to the invader camp alive, I'd already killed them myself or would in the next couple of days.

What a strange orphanage my home had become.

Clearly I wasn't going to turn Allora in, though how or why I'd come incontrovertibly to that conclusion I couldn't have said. The simplest answer would be to blame Bjartur. The implication of his sleeping position was manifest. He'd appointed himself her defender, even against me. Bjartur had never defied me, at least not in anything more serious than who got the last hot sauce packet. And I'd never defied him. I didn't think I was capable of it. My trust in the dragon far exceeded my trust in any person or institution or idea, even my own. Where Bjartur went, I would follow.

Somehow our positions had reversed, but the balance of power remained equitable. We were what we were. Inseparable.

I had to hide Allora. This was harder than it sounds. Sure, there were the woods, but my little compound had cameras installed everywhere. On the gate, on the fences, on the outside of the house. Smuggling Allora out of the house unseen was all but impossible.

Hiding her inside was equally troublesome. The housekeeper would be here in the morning after I left. I couldn't guarantee there was any corner she wouldn't poke. Not just that, but regardless of Allora's remarkable discipline today, I couldn't expect a child to remain still and hidden in some cramped place for hours on end. And while some weeks I spent far more time at home than at the Justice Center, this was not going to be one of those weeks.

I crunched on a sliver of ice. It wasn't as if these seditionists, whoever they were, had chosen some closet genius to implicate. I considered myself a reasonably intelligent person, but I was hardly a mastermind of subterfuge. I lived the most predictable, mundane existence possible. I could see where that made me an attractive choice for someone no one would suspect, but it likewise made me very ill-suited to the game they were playing.

I had the uncomfortable feeling that I and these faceless new allies of mine read too many of the same books. It's all good fun when some protagonist rises to the occasion by tapping into some unguessed-at reserves of daring, courage, and wit, but there's a reason those books are primarily found in the fiction section. Even the boldest of battlefield heroes have generally had some kind of training. I doubted jigsaw puzzles, forest strolls, and Victorian whodunits had well-prepared me for what this task demanded.

I wasn't too worried on my own account. I didn't *want* to die, certainly. There were still far too many warm sunsets, unfinished novels, and good cheeses for me to opt out voluntarily. Still, I understood the mechanisms of death far more intimately than the average person. I think for most people, the fear of death largely derives from the unknown. Will they be afraid? Will they be in pain? Will they be alone?

An execution at the hands of the state, my certain fate if I were caught, negated all such questions. Sure, it was possible the state would be tempted to make some sort of example of me. Not a public spectacle, certainly. Part of the mechanism of my business was that it was carried on thoroughly out of the town square and away from the sensibilities of the general public. That didn't mean the Justice Center mightn't want a bit of a show for the sake of discouraging any other executioners from making a mistake like mine, though.

But I had the grace of not just having been seen, once in my life, but living every day in the state of being seen, thanks to Bjartur. I wasn't afraid of leaving any piece of myself behind. If I were executed, whatever brief discomforts might precede the moment, I knew the peace and wholeness into which my soul would swiftly slip. I'd seen it, felt it, in the last breath of every person I helped move on.

No, what worried me was what would become of Bjartur. Although his fondness and fealty to our little newcomer was unmistakable, the dragon wouldn't actually imprint on anyone else in his lifetime. I didn't know for sure what the response of the state would be to his predicament without me, but I couldn't imagine any outcome that wouldn't end with him suffering a far worse death than mine. Not just dying alone, but living alone, had to be the worst of all possible realities for a creature who had never experienced emotional solitude in his entire existence. I definitely couldn't see the Justice Center allowing him to live in the wild, among other dragons, if such creatures still existed out of our reach.

So for Bjartur's sake, I had to do the best I could, well-equipped for the task or not.

And now I had Morrigan to consider as well. Although we had only just met, it seemed impossible to accept the possibility that she might be shuffled off to some stranger for display or dinner. I even fancied the dragon eggs would feel some dereliction if my pastorage was exchanged for another. Getting caught was not an option.

Try as I might, though, no brilliant plan emerged from the dusty rickets of my brain.

9

When I woke the next morning, a hot little body was curled up against my back, and it wasn't Bjartur. He was sitting atop Morrigan's tank, peering upside down at her as she floated nearby, her tentacles fluttering in his direction.

I turned my head to check the door, but it was still closed. Bjartur must have somehow persuaded Allora of the importance of keeping my bedroom door shut after she had snuck inside. Maybe I was paranoid, but especially after watching Morrigan dispatch that crab last night, I didn't want to risk finding out what she'd think of dragon eggs. Some octopuses could manage just fine out of water for short periods of time, after all.

I slid out of bed and shuffled into my everyday uniform of jeans and a t-shirt. I was fond of color, so my closet was filled with batik print t-shirts and richly dyed paisley and tartan sweaters. I never understood the so-called professional penchant for monochromatic suits and dresses. How did bleak and drab come to be associated with good-at-your-job? One more perk of being an executioner: I was exempt from office dress codes.

Allora slept on, undisturbed. I supposed she had learned to sleep in any kind of circumstances as an invader, so something as innocuous as me sliding out of bed would hardly trouble her. I mumbled a cheerless good morning to Bjartur – cheer arrived with the day's second cup of coffee – and headed out to check on our clutch.

I laid my cheek along the eggs' pulsing sides. I could feel them shifting inside the soft pearlescent shells, could hear their song rise as they acknowledged me. I rolled them over, murmuring the same sort of random nonsense with which I usually greeted them. In the midst of my current upheaval, there was a quiet consolation, a sort of peace in their serene growth. Dragons are unhurried creatures. Spending a decade inside a shell, wrapped in tuneful expectancy, they can fly from the moment they are born. Humans are always rushing from one milestone to the next, pushing themselves to achieve as fast as they can before their bones rot, but dragons are content to give every undertaking its own space. Unlike us, they don't begrudge time's incursions; they greet him as a friend, the companion none of us can outrun however hard we try.

I wasn't the giddiest of people first thing in the morning, but I was no late sleeper either. I enjoyed the moments of grace-drenched solitude found only at dawn. Soon enough I would be thigh-deep in other souls. Mornings were just me and my charges. I had plenty of time and a sweet tooth, so I made French toast and sugar-crusted bacon for breakfast. As I suspected would be the case, Allora might sleep through the second coming but not through the smell of bacon. She came creeping out of the bedroom with Bjartur perched precariously on her head.

I motioned her to a plate piled high with toast and bacon and shoved the butter and syrup in her direction. "Eat," I said. "We need to talk about what we're going to do today."

She started to scoop the bread unceremoniously into her mouth, but I couldn't permit that kind of sacrilege. "No," I explained, pouring the syrup into her plate and slathering on the butter. "Like this. And with a fork. Much better."

Bjartur hopped foot to foot, and I opened the kitchen door for him so he could partake of his morning constitutional. Almost immediately I heard the abbreviated *eep* of a grasshopper who had been loudly greeting the sun without a care. I grinned.

"So here's the deal," I told Allora between my own bites. "I have to go to work. I can't stay here with you. When I leave, other people will come here. Sometimes it's just one person, but it could be more. I don't know when they'll get here or how long they'll stay. These people are your enemies. They can't know you are here."

Allora's big eyes watched me as she chewed. She seemed to understand me, so I went on.

"Stay away from the windows. Don't ever, ever open the curtains. The front door will be locked, so when you hear someone come to the house, go very quietly to my room and hide under the bed until they're gone. You can't make a sound."

Yep. That was my grand diabolical plan: Hide under the bed.

I had actually checked under there last night. And although the edges of the hardwood floor under the bed were clearly vacuumed, a wonderful little rectangle populated by dust bunnies stood sacrosanct in the middle. I'd never been so grateful for someone else's cut corners. And the bedskirt guaranteed Allora wouldn't be visible, as long as the housekeeper had no reason to bend over and look.

I know what you're thinking. This plan, if you even want to dignify it with the name, relied heavily on a lot of variables over which I had zero control. Allora had to obey me about staying away from the windows so the gatekeeper or perimeter guards wouldn't spot her. She had to be paying attention when the housekeeper drove up to the house. She had to be quiet and perfectly still until the housekeeper left. The housekeeper had to be as unconcerned about the minutiae of her duties as she usually was. And Allora had to have gotten the gist of my directions in the first place.

All fair points. But what other option did I have? Any effort to smuggle her out of the house would have been noticed by the guards. Just bringing home the file case was aberration enough.

Follow that up with yet another heavy, suspicious package being spirited away somewhere on the grounds, and there was sure to be some investigation. And unfortunately, I was a fairly neat person. Not fond of clutter, I didn't have any untouched heaps or perilous closets in which I could squirrel Allora away.

Luckily for me, sadly for her, Allora seemed to have acquired numerous clandestine skills and a gift for silence. If she could survive yesterday's ordeal, today would be a piece of cake. Just thinking about the choking heat and darkness of that cramped little case made me want to hyperventilate.

Speaking of which, the child desperately needed a bath. That would have to wait until tonight. Assuming there was a tonight, for either of us.

Allora, for her part, simply nodded and finished her plate. I couldn't decide if her equanimity was reassuring or troubling. I needed to leave a note asking the housekeeper to pick up a new toothbrush when she brought the groceries. That wouldn't be weird, would it? A red flag, so soon after Allora's disappearance? Did the housekeeper report all my requests back to the Justice Center so they could scan them for irregularities? There had to be receipts, at least. Maybe no one looked at those but the accountant. I could hope.

I tried and failed to remember the last time I had asked for a new toothbrush. Surely the fact I couldn't remember was a good sign. It had to be time for an update. I scribbled out the note and left it on the refrigerator, adding that she was welcome to just get an economy pack if that would be easier. I figured bulk toothbrushes would be less suspicious than one more.

I showed Allora my bookshelves and the jigsaw puzzle I had laid out. I doubted if she could read in English, but my history, geology, and biology sections featured quite a few books heavy in photography. I pulled out a few I thought might hold her interest and left them stacked on the coffee table.

"My bedroom door has to stay shut at all times. You can talk to the eggs, but don't touch them. And don't touch the tank in my room."

Listing aloud all the rules Allora had to follow was stressing me out. Was it even possible for a child her age to obey all this? Desperately I wished I could stay home, or leave Bjartur behind, but that couldn't happen.

Why, I thought furiously, why had these ridiculous rebels chosen me as their collaborator? I couldn't imagine a worse option. And Shovel – Shovel, of all people, had to know the constraints under which I lived. The level of surveillance that was my daily existence.

My mouth dropped suddenly. How had I not considered it before? There was no love lost between Fiske's assistant and me. What if she had simply set me up? What if there was no expectation that Allora would be successfully hidden away? What if the whole point was to watch me fail and do away with me – and by extension, do away with Allora?

I pictured a grim look of satisfaction on Shovel's flat, pinched face as she watched me being detained and dragged away. That made more sense than anything.

Allora had immediately settled down on the floor and was poring over a photo book of volcanoes. I stared at her greasy little head.

If I was right, then killing her was my only chance at survival. Even then, I might well be discovered in the process of disposing the body. The opportunity to turn her in had come and gone; I had no viable excuse for delaying notification of the Justice Center till this morning.

As if he sensed the direction of my thoughts (and he probably did,) Bjartur tapped impatiently at the kitchen door. I opened it, and he strutted importantly across the floor to his new ward, looking over her arm as if he, too, were fascinated by volcanoes. His little malachite belly was distended with his morning meal. *Comfort food*, I thought waspishly. No doubt the interfering little bugger was stress eating. At least he was as anxious as me.

He needn't have been concerned. Maybe I was simply bored with

the monotony of my life. Maybe I was intrigued by my own inexplicable connection to this one other person in the world I'd ever met
who was like me. Maybe I was too loyal to Bjartur to break his heart
that way. Whatever the reason, I was going to let this strange chain
of possibilities play out. For once, I didn't know how my day
would end.

10

I hauled the file case, loaded with stacks of old magazines, down the drive. I had no way of knowing if this morning's driver would be the same as last night's, but I didn't want to rouse any suspicions about the change in weight. I told myself I was being paranoid, that I wasn't garnering nearly as much attention as I was trying to account for, but the assurances tasted like lies.

At any rate, the driver's face registered no change of emotion behind the dark glasses as he hefted the case into the trunk. Bjartur and I climbed into the back seat and tried to look bored as we drove into town. Like every morning, the driver didn't say a word. No note had waited for us on the seat today. I wondered frantically if that was good news or bad.

I was keenly aware of the soul now sharing a space with me. Being with Allora, even just for an evening, had permitted me a rare luxury I couldn't recall having experienced before. Anytime I was around other people, I had to maintain a fierce discipline over my own senses to keep from seeing them as they truly were. Having been trained for it from the time I was very young, the instinct was reflexive now, and dropping that defense for the soon-to-be-executed required far more effort than maintaining it. Allora, however, had such impressive defenses of her own that I could simply exist in her presence without constant maintenance of my walls. I hadn't realized it last night, in the midst of all the general terror and upheaval her appearance created, but in the car it occurred to me I had actually been more relaxed around Allora than I had been around any other human being since my training began, decades and decades ago.

It was the most peculiar peace. Rather a paradoxical one. Allora was the only human being whose soul didn't tug and pull and buzz and hum with its constant ache for attention, but then, she was the only one who might get me killed. So while she demanded nothing, she was likely going to cost me everything.

By the time we pulled up at the Justice Center, my stomach had mostly stopped protesting the day's stress. I had nearly convinced myself it was going to be just another day at the office when I saw the line at the security entrance.

It wasn't much a of a line. Not many people used the same entrance I did, so just three or four people were waiting there this morning. But I rarely met even one other person here, so my nerves immediately took up their jangling again. The poor driver had to summon his nerve to yell after me and remind me to retrieve my file case before heading in.

Bjartur settled into his harness on my back, nuzzling my neck under my hair in unspoken solidarity. I accepted the strength he offered and tried to look mildly irritated as the line shuffled forward. One of the benefits of being an executioner that no one thinks to mention is one's complete exemption from small talk, so at least I didn't have to stumble through that painful exercise. In fact, the woman in line in front of me edged as close as she could to the man in front of her to avoid any unnecessary proximity. With significant effort, I resisted the urge to fill the space she left out of sheer contrariness. I was going to need all the good karma I could scrape together to survive the escapade I'd been roped into.

Random acts of meanness toward strangers would not increase my tally.

Finally I was next in line and actually inside the doors. Three security officers instead of one manned the post. Apparently they were patting everyone down as well as searching their belongings by hand in addition to the scanner. My heart hammered in my chest like a drunken dwarf in a gold mine. Bjartur's humming increased, ever so slightly.

The facility was on a higher alert than I'd ever seen. Obviously Allora's disappearance had to have triggered this. But what else might have happened? Had her abduction only been one piece of a much larger conspiracy? I was so sheltered from information outside of my immediate person, the city could be on fire and I wouldn't know until the smoke reached my lungs.

If I were Shovel or someone like her, no doubt I could have engaged the officers in some casual good-morning chatter, extracted some nugget of information from them. But I never spoke to them. Hardly even acknowledged them. Changing my pattern on this of all mornings could not possibly be a wise decision. So I kept my lips tightly closed, pushing the file case in their direction as I sashayed through the scanner as nonchalantly as possible.

I stepped toward the officer who'd been conducting pat searches, but he shuddered slightly and motioned me on. Another officer unzipped the case and looked at me quizzically.

"Magazines?"

I shrugged. I'd come up with an answer for this earlier. "One of the upstairs ladies wants them. Some kind of art project for her kid."

He nodded, not looking any less confused but still unconcerned, and rezipped the case. He stepped back as I seized the handle and pulled it behind me. It took a real force of will to not look back and see if they were watching me, or if they'd moved on to the next person in line. It occurred to me that if I were cleverer and more motivated, no doubt I could have used my status as executioner and general Dread Lady to smuggle all sorts of contraband in here over the years. Alas. Wasted potential.

My tension only increased as I moved through the building and rode the elevator to my floor. I saw lots of unfamiliar faces, and people moved through the halls with tight expressions, downcast eyes, and shuffling feet that seemed to be on the verge of breaking into a run at any moment. I asked myself, if I were innocent, would I go straight to Fiske's office and demand an explanation of what was happening, or would I go straight to my own office as if it were just another day?

Probably anyone else would have gone to Fiske, but I knew that wasn't my style. Whatever was happening in the building would have no impact on my duties. Nothing had an impact on my duties. As long as the state stood, people had to die. Sometimes just a few people, sometimes a shitload, like this week.

A shitload. I tried the word out loud, decided it had a lovely, meaty feel to it that perfectly suited the deluge of cases I'd been assigned. You may have never thought about it, but swearing is a weirdly communal habit. The words function as a sort of rebellion or outrage against the mundane – an extraordinary pain, an extraordinary anger, an extraordinary surprise, an extraordinary joy. For instance, stubbing one's toe satisfies the first three of those in one. But there's not much satisfaction in expressing rebellion or outrage to yourself. Even when a person does use profanity alone, they nearly always look around to see if anyone heard it, or maybe they direct it to the sky or to some lurking deity. At any rate, the words tend to fall flat when you're always solitary. But I liked to think that if I were ever a woman of the world, I'd swear like a sailor.

I wondered if Bjartur felt the same, if dragons had their own expletives only other dragons understood and those words' salt had lost their savor for him. I hoped not. That felt sad, as if a disused branch of language were a lost limb.

"Shitload," I muttered again, opening the door to my office. It was the lone room in the building that appeared untouched by whatever crisis was appearing—still as stuffy and dour as ever, with no sign of any panicked rifling. Admittedly, there wasn't much to rifle. My desk drawers were mostly used for emergency candy supplies and hot sauce packets for Bjartur. A single file sat haphazardly on the edge, as if it had been flung there. I wondered what had happened to the dozens of executions I'd had scheduled for today when I left last night.

Bjartur had hopped out of his harness and was strolling around the floor in that weird, wobbling gait dragons have, adding further to the indignity by stretching out one knobby-kneed leg at a time and cracking his toes. He'd been as stressed as me. We were alpha predators, the two of us, whether we wanted to be or not, and stress was an uncommon sensation for us. Uncommon and decidedly unpleasant. Adrenaline junkies seemed more incomprehensible than ever to me. Who would willingly and repeatedly put themselves in a position where their life was at risk? I did not like it, not at all.

So why was I doing this? I thought of Allora, pictured her lying silently under the bed listening to the footsteps of a housekeeper whose name I did not know. It wasn't the pangs of a suddenly overactive conscience, because I saw nothing wrong and much good in my calling. It wasn't the desire for something new and different in my life. Bjartur and I lived in perfect contentment. But sometimes, I was learning, contentment could be stagnation.

Inexplicably, Allora felt like a sister to me. Family was a sleeping ghost in the back corners of my mind, so long still and silent now that I'd all but forgotten what it meant. When I'd lost my parents, the teachers made no effort to make up for the absence. That part of my life – belonging, loving, expecting, accepting – was simply over. Allora somehow prodded that old ghost awake, made me feel a connection that inexplicably overrode all other considerations, even self-preservation. I baffled myself.

My hand went to the lone file on my desk. Normally I never looked before the execution was complete, but nothing this morning was normal. According to what Fiske said yesterday, today should have seen another avalanche of files waiting for me, but there was only one. Dread shuddered through me.

I flipped it open. A name floated up: *Bedelia Carter*. Why was that name familiar? I wondered. Then my eyes moved to the photo paper-clipped to the page.

It was a face I recognized immediately.

Shovel.

My stomach heaved.

11

A cursory knock on the door had Bjartur and me both jumping at the same time, and Fiske strode in.

He looked terrible. I could only guess from its crumpled and soiled state that his suit was the same he'd been wearing yesterday. Fiske never looked exactly jolly to see me, but this morning his expression was downright grim. I suspected the harried look in his eyes was fed not by stress but by raw, desperate fear.

"Good," he said shortly. "You're here."

I shrugged, trying for nonchalant. "Aren't I always? It is nine o'clock."

His eyes flitted toward the manila file on my desk, then flitted away. He gestured toward it— a brief, aborted movement. He looked reluctant to break the air, to take up space, even as he forced himself onward.

"Have you looked at your appointment?"

I shook my head. "I never look till after. Doesn't mesh with my practice."

Fiske's lips twisted with the usual scorn. He might use an executioner, might pander to one and even fear one, but he despised them, all the same. The ineffable aspects of our task, what couldn't be quantified or slid neatly into a checkbox on a computer screen, unnerved and discomfited him. And the human response to anything uncomfortable is most often contempt.

"You'll want to look this time. Today's work will be somewhat out of the ordinary."

I nodded disinterestedly and opened the file. Shovel's face, incongruously bright with first-day-of-work nerves and cheer, beamed up at me. I read her name aloud slowly. "Bedelia Carter? What is this about?"

Lying is like swearing. It's communal, too. I suppose a person can lie to themselves, in the absence of any other influence, but why bother? If there's no one else around to levy judgment, peace with oneself requires no effort at all. It's only when other people insist you need to be/look/feel/think a certain way, that the mind rallies to pretend that it already does.

My world, as I've told you, is small. It's basically Bjartur and me. Bjartur wouldn't be fooled by any artifice, nor would he require any. He doesn't care how soft my belly is or whether I read high enough literature or if I plant the right flowers. As for my work, that has always been an extension of my identity. Shorting my duties would be shorting myself. And when it comes to interpersonal relationships – well, you already know I have no qualms about honesty there. Life is too short to waste pretending you like people you don't. It's also too short to waste time pretending people are more important to you than they are. So dissembling is not an art I've ever had cause to cultivate.

It was a deficiency of which I was suddenly, keenly, aware as I attempted to shift my face into what I hoped was both ignorance and surprise. Maybe horror? Maybe not. After all, Fiske knew I'd never liked Shovel.

But I'd have still been startled to conduct her execution,

wouldn't I, if I knew nothing about what had happened? I thought so. Horrified? Probably not. Was that still another deficiency? Was I less professional and more psychopathic than I'd suspected?

Nonsense. This was an anomaly. Nothing about this situation was typical. There was no blueprint for emotional range here. I would have to wing it.

Fiske seemed to be buying it. So far, at least.

"There was a security breach last night. Our investigators discovered that Ms. Carter was implicated. She was helpful enough to give up her accomplices, with only one stipulation: that you not be her executioner. Obviously she must have co-conspirators among the other executioners or possibly their staff. At any rate, we couldn't take the risk. I know it's unusual for you to have to execute someone you know personally, but I'm hoping I can count on you."

I'd never actually wished the woman dead, but I had to admit, two days ago this would have been a much easier question to answer than it was now. Still, I replied with alacrity.

"Of course. Have I ever not done my job?"

"No, no, you've always been absolutely reliable." Fiske honest-to-goodness wrung his hands, a sight which heightened my anxiety considerably. "This is just a little out of the ordinary."

"I'm well aware that the dragon and I offer a far more humane passage than any other people could expect. I've no scruples about my work. It's an act of compassion, not a curse."

"Yes. Yes. Quite. She should be so grateful." Fiske rubbed his hands briskly together like a slightly chilly villain in a bad cartoon. "I'll leave you to it then. You're welcome to go home after that — we've transported the remaining invaders to other facilities."

I raised my eyebrows. "I thought you were worried the other executioners might have been compromised? And what exactly happened last night, anyway?"

"Those decisions are above my pay grade. The Council knows what they're doing. I've said more than I should have, anyway. The security breach has nothing to do with your job. You just mind your eggs."

"What about the accomplices she gave up? Won't I be executing them also?"

Fiske shrugged. "They're still being interrogated. We'll send a car for you in the morning, like always, if we need you."

With that he stepped backwards out of the door. I couldn't tell if he was anxious to end the conversation without giving away anything unnecessary or if it was just his usual discomfort around Bjartur and me. In either case, I was glad he was gone. I eyed my chair wistfully, wishing I could sink into it for a moment. Lying, it turned out, even by omission, was stressful work. I didn't under-stand why anyone would do it voluntarily. From everything I'd read, anything that started with a lie ended in a catastrophe. I had no illu-sions and no real hopes about my own circumstances. Something about delaying the inevitable, though, was apparently irresistible. If a person knows they have ten seconds to live, they will do anything to keep breathing through every one of those seconds.

Bjartur fluttered awkwardly up onto the desk and eyed me expectantly. It was no good trying to procrastinate. That would only make things harder for all of us in the end, not least of all Shovel. Dread of death is always a thousand times worse than death itself, especially death by dragon. I tilted my head and extended my arm so Bjartur could clamber into his harness. I sorted my features into what I thought was their usual order and strode out the doorway as if it were any typical morning.

I wondered briefly if I should start referring to her in my mind as Bedelia instead of Shovel. The effort felt impractical, given that she was about to drop out of existence on this side of things, but we were allies of a sort now, weren't we? Even if our bizarre conspiracy had been foisted on me against my will, I had consented to it in the end. And I had no doubt she had her reasons for manipulating Fiske into ensuring that I would be her executioner. I only hoped it wasn't because she thought there was some chance I'd fail my duty.

Bjartur and I hadn't been in the execution room more than three minutes when the door buzzed and a guard escorted her in. They must have been watching the cameras for my arrival. Shovel – my brain tripped over Bedelia, so I gave that right up – looked considerably worse than most of my subjects. Generally speaking, the whole point of this process was a humane solution to society's problems, so torture wasn't standard. Over the course of the last few decades, though, I'd had my share of political prisoners who sometimes looked a little worse for wear, invaders who'd put up a fight, that sort of thing. But Shovel appeared to have been systematically worked over. Her escort practically carried her to one of the soft chairs and settled her into it with uncommon care. His expression struck me: jaw tightly clenched, mouth twisted. His eyes flashed to mine for a split second. I saw contempt shining there, but whether it was intended for me or directed at himself, I couldn't tell. Maybe both.

It's hard, when you're consistently told your entire purpose is mercy, to bear witness to deliberate cruelty in your name. I didn't fault him.

On the other hand, it made me doubt him. Had Shovel really given up all her accomplices? She hadn't given up me. At least, I found it highly unlikely she had. It was still possible Fiske and the Council were playing some preposterous long game, trying to lure me into a sense of false security. Maybe even this moment itself was part of a test. I didn't think so, though.

I sat down across from her and lowered my arm out of sheer habit. Bjartur clambered out of his harness and walked down to the carpet. Shovel had closed her eyes as she was lowered into the chair, whether in pain or exhaustion I wasn't sure. At the sound of Bjartur's creaky wings, she opened them. To my surprise, she leaned forward gingerly and let Bjartur rub his bony head against her cupped palm.

"Who's going to get your hot sauce for you today, little fella?" she said softly.

I tried not to gape.

My blind spots are considerable. I know this, but normally I don't care. As a seer, protecting myself from the constant bombardment of passing spirits takes precedence over general discernment. The toll would be exhausting otherwise. And it's not as if street-smarts are a necessary part of my repertoire. I'm protected from most of the nastiness other people face on a daily basis: emotional manipulation, political maneuvering, run-of-the-mill deceit. It's quite easy for the few people with whom I interact to fool me when it comes to their nature, their intentions, their motivations. I figure if they want to go to all that trouble, I may as well play along. It costs me nothing, and presumably it matters to them for some reason. Bjartur is the only real relationship in my life. Maybe Morrigan will change that.

Nonetheless, it was always a shock when I ran into one of those weird reversals of human nature. This woman I had always found so irascible and petty and dour, sitting here looking like a hammered piece of meat, cooing and petting my dragon – the dragon that was about to end her life, the dragon I'd always thought she'd loathed – had completely bamboozled me in so many ways.

Made sense, I supposed. After all, she was apparently a spy of some sort, a secret operative for a shadowy group of people whose motivations I couldn't begin to unravel. Subterfuge had to have been a strong point of hers.

Bjartur bumped his head insistently against her palm and hummed happily to himself as she scratched down his neck. "It's okay, you know," she said, her attention still seemingly directed at Bjartur.

I took her meaning. Suddenly, unexpectedly, this was harder than I thought it would be. I'd wondered if she would beg. If she'd give me away at the last minute to the watching cameras. More than that, I realized that somehow, I'd been expecting her to have some elaborate escape already planned. That this would only be a bit of theatre and her people, whoever they were, would save her.

But no. It was as simple as it looked. She intended to keep my secret to the end. And this was the end.

I pulled my chair forward so that our knees were nearly touching. She leaned back, and I lifted Bjartur to the arm of her chair. Some people liked to hold the dragon in their laps, but I didn't think she had an unbruised inch on her body. Bjartur stepped closer, gently nuzzling her shoulder.

Her gaze met mine.

I'd never had to execute someone I knew before. I'd never had to consciously lay aside the trappings of self with which they draped themselves, but in that moment, they fell away effortlessly. I forgot Shovel entirely. Shovel was a construct I'd created. I saw Bedelia.

Souls are knitted together with a language, but it's not a tongue I speak. Perhaps it's the language we've all forgotten, the one we had to translate into what we call our mother tongue when we were infants. It's more like music than these abrupt grunts and ejaculations of sound that we name words. Still, words are all that remain to me now to express what I see when I allow myself to truly look into a person.

The nearest metaphor I can offer is of water. Some people are warm tropical waters, sunlit and sparkling, their depths filled alike with stunning wonders and lurking dangers. Some are murky swamps, where life and death swallow each other in an endless cycle that gives birth to rot and bloom in equal measure. Some, by the time I meet them, are mere icy puddles, absent of light or life, only rippling when disturbed from the outside.

If I'd still been on the outside, I'd have been surprised by her warmth. I'd have expected cold depths from her. But when with the soul, there is no surprise, no expectation, no self. Only other.

I sank into her, effortless as always. A warm deep pool, bounded by rocks, scant yards from the tumbling terminus of a waterfall. Aquatic ferns drifted in the current, refuge and camouflage for strange and fantastic creatures who sinuously swam in a complicated pattern that prodded but did not quite wake the memory. The floor of the little pool glittered with quartz and agate, garnet and gold, sieved and sifted in a fine black grit. Shafts of sunshine flickered, ladders of light whose gleaming flashes more blinded than illu-minated.

Tiny, velvety mosses and patient snails clung to the underbelly of the rocks who made up the pool's verge. As I came back to myself, I could taste the warm, surging animus of the mountain river; I could feel the smooth weight and strength of those stones against my hand.

Bedelia's gaze still held mine. Without a blink, I wordlessly prompted Bjartur to his task. His green head flashed forward, his teeth sinking into the bruised flesh, and Bedelia's eyes fell closed. Her body slumped in the chair.

Bjartur fluttered over to my lap as I leaned back. Executions were necessarily draining, but I felt exceptionally depleted. And excep-tionally foolish, but not in a humorous way. In a stupid, blind way.

My perception of Bedelia (shame cowered as the name Shovel rose to mind) had been so far off, it was beyond preposterous. It wasn't as if I fancied myself an expert on human nature – quite the opposite. I mostly ignored human nature, apart from the necessities of my work. I had neither friends nor enemies. I only ever needed to trust anyone to the extent that they continued to provide me food and shelter, which had never been in question. Identifying and comprehending the vagaries of people held no interest for me. And Bedelia Carter had been doing all she could not to be perceived as anything more than a mildly obstructive assistant to the executive.

Still, if I was that far off about Bedelia, what else was I wrong about? Doubt, I'd imagined, was something a person outgrew. My life had been all certainties for decades. At least, I thought it had been.

Questioning my realities brought me abruptly back into myself. I couldn't afford to lapse into some maudlin philosophical funk while her body cooled. That was not typical behavior for an executioner at all, and now more than ever I had to appear impeccably typical. Sensing my distress, Bjartur clawed his way up to my shoulders as I stood, wrapping himself snugly around my neck instead of dropping into his harness. I crossed the room and rang the button to let the escort know he could dispose of the body.

"Home for us, then, boy," I murmured, scratching around the dragon's sensitive earholes. "Everything's normal. Everything's fine."

12

Morrigan drifted to meet my hand on the glass. Allora stood beside me, her bony shoulder pressing into my own. Already I'd learned she had a hunger for touch. What an unfortunate appetite. I'd been alone with Bjartur for so long, I'd all but forgotten what it was to experience human touch. It certainly never occurred to me to reach for it.

Even my octopus seemed more needy than I'd anticipated. Clearly her curiosity had overcome her latent suspicion. I felt quite confident I had Allora to thank for that.

"Been playing with the octopus much today?" I asked, not expecting an answer. Allora's dark eyes searched mine, and she laid her palm on the glass alongside mine.

Yeah. She'd definitely been coaxing Morrigan from her refuge while I was gone. Hopefully she hadn't fed her all the crabs. I could see one poor doomed critter popping an anxious eye out from behind the rocks. Obviously Allora had fed Morrigan enough that she'd lost interest and allowed one an extra day – or hour (how often did octopuses need to eat?) – to live.

I twisted around and shot a glance toward the tank in the corner of the room. There were at least some crabs left. I couldn't bring myself to scold Allora for the effort. What kind of person wouldn't feed a hungry octopus?

I stole another look at the little girl whose survival had suddenly become my responsibility. Bjartur lounged lazily along her neck and shoulders as if he belonged there. Something like jealousy twinged in my chest, and just as quickly evaporated. Bjartur might love a thousand people, but we would always belong to each other. Granted, I'd never seen him take to anyone else for longer than it took for me to see them and him to kill them, but still. Some things were just true. And Bjartur and me belonging to each other – that was an unassailable truth. No matter who he cuddled. No matter who he refused to kill.

I had to hope Allora's continued presence here and the absence of any armed guards awaiting me meant our poor little ruse of hiding her under the bed had been good enough. We'd need something better long-term. Wouldn't we?

My head hurt. I was not meant to be a super spy. I was barely meant to be an executioner. Luckily for all of us, my particular skill set had dovetailed nicely with the undeniable perks of the position and Bjartur's own irresistibility. After all, what teenager could resist a dragon of their own? Certainly not me. From the moment Bjartur had imprinted on me, I'd been willing to do whatever was necessary to keep us together. Then again, maybe that whole idea is too human-centric; maybe *I* imprinted on Bjartur when he came tap-tapping out of that magical singing eggshell instead of the other way around.

Regardless, from my first sighting of that tiny little jewel-winged creature, I'd have done anything, absolutely anything, to keep us together. To keep him safe. My fosters had warned me he couldn't survive without me.

But for the first time since I'd watched that iridescent shell shimmer and shatter, I doubted.

In the wild, Bjartur would have imprinted on his own dragon-mother. Or father. I didn't know anything about the familial patterns of wild dragons. As far as I knew, there wasn't such a thing anymore. But if by nature, dragons did imprint on their parents, they had to be able to survive the rending of that imprint. Didn't they? Wouldn't they need to go out into the world, find their own mates, hatch their own eggs, raise their own dragonlings? It couldn't be right that a dragon perished when the imprint failed. Could it?

Equal parts frustrated that I hadn't asked the question before and that I didn't know the answer, I flicked Bjartur on his bony ridged spine. He huffed a faint puff of sulfur in my direction and closed his eyes, utterly untroubled by my distress.

I told myself that was fine. It wasn't as if we needed to have the same response to every stimuli, every time. The fact that we generally had up until now was just a convenient coincidence.

Assuming, a nasty voice buried in my brain piped up, *he hasn't been fooling you all along.* Maybe even the seeming convergences of the past were only a façade.

Maybe Bjartur, like Shovel, *like Bedelia,* only pretended to be who they seemed.

Bjartur raised his head at that thought. Unable to stop myself, I extended my hand toward him. He opened his kittenish mouth, and I placed my forefinger on his lower jaw. He closed his upper teeth over my digit and bit down, just enough to bruise but not break the flesh. I chuckled tearfully, taking his meaning as effortlessly as always.

You're an idiot.

Allora seemed oblivious to our unspoken exchange, her attention focused on the octopus floating on the other side of the glass. I needed to feed her, I realized when my own belly growled. She'd tended to Morrigan, but based on the pristine state of the rest of the house, I didn't think she'd had anything to eat herself while I was gone. I had no experience with children, but still I didn't imagine even the most responsible of them could manage to fix themselves food and leave no trace of it behind. I probably couldn't do that myself. A lifetime of being cleaned up after doesn't lend itself to fussiness.

I was going to leave Allora and Bjartur with Morrigan, but the girl trailed after me into the kitchen. Tired of being alone, I supposed, although personally I'd have preferred the company of an octopus to that of most any person. The dragon eggs sang softly from their nest, unperturbed. Even with all the uncertainty and fear of this day, their sole purpose remained unchanged: live. Live and grow and wait for their moment. Whatever became of me or Allora or even Bjartur, they would continue their task. I wasn't sure if that thought was hopeful or nihilistic.

We had jerk chicken nachos for dinner. My world might be small, but my diet was well-traveled. I had shelves of cookbooks and loved to try new dishes. The housekeeper probably dreaded my grocery lists, but she'd never yet failed to bring back everything on them. Or he. Housekeepers could be hes. Not in Victorian novels, maybe, but surely in real life. I was fairly certain the current iteration actually was a she, but I couldn't be sure. I never paid attention to the signatures on the refrigerator notes. What difference did it make to me?

Allora ate steadily without complaint. I'd made the food as mild as possible just in case and loaded up plenty of extra cheese, but that was more for my own sake than hers. I had an idea for how I could hide her long-term, but she'd have to make do with staying under the bed for now. I daren't risk any unusual activity showing up on the cameras if the Council decided to review them. So there was definitely no way for her to join Bjartur and me on our evening walk. Still, I could lay some groundwork.

While we munched, I scribbled out a note for the housekeeper to bring me some seeds and bulbs and raised bed supplies. I'd been gardening – poorly – for several years now, so that would ring no alarm bells.

"You stay here," I told Allora as Bjartur and I finished eating and stood to go outside. I don't know if she understood my words, but she took my meaning. I couldn't help feeling like a monster at the look in her eyes. That look was the reason I'd never wanted a bird or a rat or a gerbil as a pet (besides the fact that Bjartur would probably eat them).

It's rather terrible, keeping any living thing in a cage. It doesn't matter if that life is feral or rabid or just plain evil. It doesn't matter if you're convinced the cage is the only thing keeping it safe. Standing on the other side of the bars with a key in your hand, a key you won't turn, does something to the human spirit. Twists it. Turns it to concrete and crumbles it. The more you walk by that locked door, the more you find yourself on the wrong side of it. And then there's that look.

It's a thousand things, that look. It's the betrayal of a confidence that should never have existed, a trust that should never have formed, based solely on the irrational expectation that a human will behave in a humane way. It's desperation, a pleading without pride. It's despair, the already-acknowledged truth that there is no out, after all. It's a craven sort of dependence, a longing for kindness from the one person holding you captive. And worst of all, it's hope.

It was the first look I saw on the face of every person I'd ever executed, before they were distracted by the wonder and terror of the dragon. Before they realized this was the last room they'd enter, that I was the last person they'd ever touch. Before they accepted that this was the very end.

So why did I get an octopus? A tank, after all, is just another sort of cage. I had lots of reasons, actually, of which I might persuade myself. A tank isn't a cage at all, it's a small sea. Without someone like me, Morrigan would have been doomed to either live out her existence entirely alone or else end up drenched in breadcrumbs and fried in oil. I felt a need to understand what Magenna had been talking about, a need that might well relate to my very survival.

Those excuses all sounded more or less passable, if not entirely convincing, but probably the truth was simply that my want overcame my scruples. It is wrong and selfish to keep something in a cage. Reasons to the contrary are beside the moral point. But I wanted the octopus, I wanted to learn what it already understood. So I was wrong, and I was selfish.

I motioned to the windows and did my best to reiterate that Allora needed to stay out of sight. It might be unlikely, but we didn't need some guard noticing a suspicious shadow moving in the house after he'd seen me heading toward the trees. I kept my sympathy well-concealed behind a stern look.

I went to the garden shed, piled up the wheelbarrow with my supplies, and covered them with a black tarp. I wheeled it over to the back door and wandered in and out of the house with armfuls of stuff I added to my barrow. Finally I trundled down the sweeping meadow toward the woods, Bjartur swooping and flying low alongside me till we reached the trees. He soared up over the canopy and disappeared on his nightly hunting trip while I headed into the dim quiet of the evening arbor.

I didn't think I needed to go far. As long as no one suspected me of anything, no one would venture one step into the forest, much less several yards. And if anyone suspected, I might as well give up entirely, because there was zero chance of me getting away with my poor subterfuge. I had no doubt that the only reason Bedelia and her mysterious compadres chose me for their plan was precisely because my loyalty was unquestionable. Suspecting me of being a rebel collaborator was like suspecting the Pope of being a moonlighting French chef who just pops by the Vatican on his off days. It simply doesn't even come to mind.

I found a little clearing that looked to do nicely. I got to work as quickly as I could, hammering boards to tree trunks and creating a sort of rafter-system of ropes on which I draped the tarp to make what I hoped was a rainproof ceiling. I had a few pavers I laid on the dirt once I raked it clear. I didn't know how squeamish Allora might be about creepy-crawlies, but I figured a little distance between her and the dirt couldn't hurt.

Ideally I'd have thrown together some actual walls, but I'd never had much need for building materials. The boards I did have were basi-cally glorified gardening stakes. Given enough time, Allora and I could scavenge enough limbs to build walls we could insulate with some-thing or other – I'd have to think about that. But maybe she wouldn't be here long enough for that. Whoever delivered her to me must have had some kind of plan. Surely they would contact me somehow.

Allora could be their problem then, and I could return to my nice, quiet, predictable schedule of executions and home suppers.

I left two blankets piled on top of the pavers. I squished a long-handled flashlight into the soft ground and taped an empty milk carton over it. That'd make a fine lamp for her once dark fell, if we decided she needed to spend nights as well as days out here. If she was scared of the dark, well, she'd likely burn right through the batteries, but luckily they were rechargeable.

I stood back and regarded my haphazard construction with satis-faction. Not bad for a first-time builder, I thought. It wasn't exactly the most comfortable of accommodations, but I told myself invaders were well-accustomed to hardship. And she'd be dry and warm enough, at least. If anything, she might get too hot in these summer days. The forest shade should help with that, I hoped.

Which reminded me: I set several bottles of water beside the "lamp." Tomorrow when I brought her out here, after the house-keeper had delivered my gardening supplies, I'd bring more creature comforts. She'd be more than fine, I told myself. Certainly safer than what would become of her if the housekeeper or one of the guards found her. Who knew what the Council had planned for her? Nothing good, I was sure of that. Why else would Bedelia have sacri-ficed her life to save some random invader's child she didn't even know?

As I came out of the forest twilight and pushed the wheelbarrow back up the hill, Bjartur swooped out of the sky and landed in the tub instead of on my shoulder, as he usually did. Clasped tightly in one little talon was a plastic tube of some sort, almost like a test tube with a cork in the end. He tapped it impatiently on the dirty metal and looked at me with expectant jeweled eyes.

I swallowed hard and forced myself to keep the same leisurely pace. Somehow, someone had gotten a message to my dragon. In all my life, such a thing had never happened. The possibility hadn't even occurred to me. My whole body thrummed with impatience and excitement, but I merely tipped my chin at Bjartur and spoke in a mutter.

"Hang on to it for now, buddy. It's not safe to show it out here. Let's wait till we get inside."

I propped the wheelbarrow beside the back door. Allora was waiting, perhaps three feet away from the glass door, peering anxiously out as she waited for us to return. Bjartur fluttered in ahead of me, dropping the canister on my favorite chair with a self-important humph. I couldn't blame him for his pomposity: being a courier for rebels wasn't something just anybody could claim.

Allora watched, bright-eyed, as I shook out a piece of paper and unrolled it.

They were never your parents, and they're not dead.

13

So surreal. I wondered if this what it felt like to be high. My back was propped against the foot of my bed, my legs spread out on the carpet in front of me. Allora leaned against my belly, her left arm holding mine against her bony little body, while she petted a tuneful Bjartur perched on her skinny thigh. Morrigan prowled the bottom of her tank as we watched her in the eerie purple aquarium light.

Allora, of course, had been the one to decide our sitting arrangement, manipulating my limbs like some sort of oversized teddy bear. Beside us, bowls of popcorn and chocolate stars offered consolation for the weirdness of the day.

Maybe I should read to the girl. That's what caretakers did, wasn't it? Read to children at night? Surely I had something appropriate on my shelves. Not that she would understand most of the words, although I was still unsure how much English she spoke. Maybe the rumble of a gentle voice and the familiarity of the ritual would be soothing enough in itself. Her own parents must have read to her, or at least told her bedtime stories.

Her own parents.

That note had staggered me more than I cared to admit. As if this situation wasn't bizarre and terrifying enough as it was, these strangers had to come after not just my present existence, but my memories, too. I wanted to insist to myself that it couldn't be true, but based on what?

Everything about my life since the alleged car accident that took their lives had been perfectly orchestrated by the state. My various fosters, though kind enough, were matter-of-fact and distant, trainers of my latent skills rather than caregivers. I was a means to an end, and none of us were deceived on that point. Was it really beyond the realm of possibility to think that my life prior to that had been an illusion manipulated for the state's purposes, too?

It had been a long time since I'd thought about my parents at any length. My eyes clung to Morrigan's rippling colors as I pictured them. We were at a park on a school day, so the playground toys were mostly deserted besides the toddlers occupying the smallest ones. Museums, zoos, playgrounds were all quieter places for us, since we could go when public school children were locked inside four walls, their bouncing thighs restrained beneath a desk. My parents were devoted to me in a way I'd since learned from reading was uncommon, so devoted that I never longed to be like the other children or missed a playmate of my own age.

On that day, that for some reason now sprang to mind full-color, Mom and Dad and I were racing each other down the three curly slides sported by this most elite of playgrounds. I could hear Mom laughing, high-pitched and breathless, could hear Dad's wild child-friendly curses as his hefty belly undid the advantage of his longer legs, could even hear the birds singing in the trees that kept the hot spring sun from being unbearable. I could feel the cool steel of the ladder under my palms, could feel my arms wrap around my once-bony knees as I curled myself up for maximum speed and leaned back before hurtling down the slide.

Morrigan settled into the crevasse behind the fake rock on the left side of the tank. Strange to think that Morrigan and all her accoutrements were only here in my bedroom through the unbending efficiency of a woman I'd killed just a few hours ago. Had Bedelia actually picked out all the rocks and plants and glittering gravel, or had she simply ordered from the octopus supply store or wherever in the world she'd gotten this extravagance and asked to have it delivered with everything an octopus might possibly need?

Morrigan had never known her parents. Her father would have died almost immediately after fertilizing her mother. Her mother would have been the fiercest of guardians as she protected her clutch of hundreds of eggs, gently agitating the water to keep currents flowing over her brood of tinies. Octopus mothers, I'd read, eschewed all sense of their own survival from the moment they laid their eggs. They stopped hunting, not even snagging the odd prey that drifted unwittingly past their den. Depending on the species, they might go as long as ten months without food. Once the eggs hatched, the mother's work was done, and she succumbed to starvation as her oblivious infants floated away on the currents.

As clever and adept as octopuses were, it was almost chilling to think how much more they might learn, might understand, if they had the benefit of a teacher. But a young octopus had to acquire alone every bit of knowledge and every skill on which their lives depended. Every octopus was an orphan.

Was I an octopus after all? Were the people I remembered as my parents only keepers? Two little sentences from some unknown, invisible stranger had cast my entire identity in doubt. How irrational was that? I knew that these rebels, whoever they were, served only their own interests. Their own violent, seditious interests. If they were willing to overthrow a state, they were surely willing to overthrow the confidence of an executioner by filling her head with half-formed conspiracies and lies. I didn't know why I was even contemplating the possibility they raised.

If I reached all the way to the back of my throat, I could still taste the grief and shock of the car accident that took them both from me on the same day. For a long while, the sadness and abandonment had been overwhelming. My parents, after all, weren't just my parents: they were my teachers, my friends, my playmates. My universe. Without them, I came completely unmoored.

My fosters had one purpose, and it wasn't comfort. It was conditioning. Everything my parents and my childhood had given me—love, affection, joy, security—were repurposed. Day after day, I was taught that my own emotions were only the tools by which I comprehended the being of others. My grief and longing for what I'd lost became the Rosetta Stone by which I translated the griefs and longings of strangers. My innate ability as a seer, something I'd never questioned as my parents encouraged and coaxed my nascent talent, emerged as a rare gift, now owed to the survival of the state.

Bjartur was the one concession to my individual identity, or so I'd imagined when we'd first met. What remained of my shredded affections by the end of every day was lavished on him, and his loyalty was absolute. Days when I had failed and failed and failed again to meet the expectations of my fosters, he loved me deeply and unreservedly. By the time I realized that he, like me, was nothing more than a pawn of the law, it only increased my devotion to the scaly little winged beast. We were islanded together in a world of unfriendly seas. It wasn't that the world was hostile to us. It was simply Other. We alone understood each other.

So I'd been divided from both the loss and the love of my parents long ago. I was familiar with it like I was familiar with stories I'd read in childhood; their details faded, but the import of their conclusion remained as the imprint of a distant emotion. I could examine the cords I'd thought so unbreakable and see if perhaps the threads were more worn than I knew, if they in fact reached far beyond the knot I'd thought ended in me.

Certainly my childhood had been unusual. It hadn't seemed so at the time. Gradually, from the more modern books I read, I realized that at least one and often both parents had jobs that kept them from home most of the time. Both my parents spent all their time with me. Our home was not large, but it was isolated on acres of property at the edge of the town where we went for groceries, library books, parks, museums, and the post office. No neighbors questioned our habits. I had no grandparents, no cousins, no aunts and uncles. It occurred to me, for the first time, that I had no knowledge of my parents' families or backgrounds at all. I'd been trained ever since their deaths to look forward, not back, at my own duty to myself, my state, and my dragons. It was as if my parents, and my parents alone, existed to nurture me in a very particular fashion right up until their deaths.

So while I had no proof, no evidence to back up the mad claim of whoever had intercepted Bjartur, I had little enough argument against it, either. Could the people I remembered and loved as Mom and Dad have been another set of fosters all along? The first set to nurture the necessary empathy and security to produce a powerful seer who wasn't also a sociopath, the second set to turn that neophyte seer into a honed and polished weapon?

I became aware that Allora and Bjartur were both snoring, Allora's a soft little-girl huffing, and Bjartur's a small rattling growl from the back of his throat. He'd rolled over onto his spine, his hind legs splayed over Allora's thigh, his wings and head lolling on mine, his pale aqua-glitter belly fearlessly exposed. I sighed. Extricating myself would be a bit of a trick.

Out my window, the late summer sun had long since sunk, and the blazing skies had submitted to the cooler blue of a moonless night. Morrigan's purple light was all that illuminated my room. I squirreled my way out from under my two charges with a fair bit of difficulty, but neither roused. I lifted Bjartur first, carrying him to sleep in the manger with the dragon eggs. Their humming comforted him, and I liked to imagine that the growing infants sensed the presence of an older brother, even if they'd be forever divorced from their own kind once they hatched. Unless, of course, they were selected for breeding, but I had no knowledge of that process. For all I knew, even that was entirely a test-tube affair.

I hefted up the sleeping Allora with every intention of carrying her out to her bed on the couch. Her wiry little black curls smooshed against my bare arm, and her weight in my arms stirred an unfamiliar protective feeling I'd have thought was limited entirely to Bjartur. Instead, I laid her in the bed and covered her with the thin sheet before opening my bedroom window and sliding in beside her.

I listened to the frogs and crickets and locusts and the quiet snores of a child I still hadn't killed and hardly slept at all.

14

The summer dawn cared little for my sleepless night. The bed beside me was empty when I rolled over, and I could hear Allora's and Bjartur's voices from the other room. I rose out of bed with the usual chorus of creaks and groans and proceeded blearily toward the coffeemaker in the kitchen. The housekeeper wouldn't arrive for a couple hours yet, so I had plenty of time to stow Allora away, eat some breakfast, and send the house-keeper out to buy my supplies as soon as she arrived.

A full 48 hours of not getting caught had irrationally boosted my self-confidence. Even more inexplicably, the whole affair had taken on an element of fun I hadn't experienced for longer than I could remember. Building a forest fortress, however shoddy, and actually having and keeping a secret suddenly seemed liked exactly the sort of thing an executioner-seer should have been doing all along. At my age, I thought whimsically, I ought to be fully transitioning into a crone.

Crones were notoriously intractable, after all, and who would want to go up against one *and* her dragon? Maybe I would embrace the rebellious life after all.

Of course, having to execute Bedelia had put a damper on things, but that was part of the daily grind of the business I was in, I tried to tell myself. It couldn't all be fun and tiddlywinks.

I was downing my second cup of coffee and beginning to think seriously about food when a knock at the back door made me jump out of my skin.

Allora froze, her dark eyes seeking mine. I made a quick motion with my hand toward my bedroom, and she nodded in perfect comprehension. She bent over and scuttled across the floor like one of Morrigan's crabs. I heard her slide across the hardwood floor under the bed. Bjartur had puffed up at the knock, craning his neck imperiously and spreading his wings as if to make himself look as imposing as possible. Now he soared across the open space to land on my shoulder.

I set my coffee cup down, willing my hands not to shake, and turned to open the door. All that sense of fun and vim I'd been bubbling with a moment before evaporated.

A small figure slipped inside so fast, I barely even saw her. She closed and locked the door behind her in a single smooth motion, then turned to face me.

I say she, but the interloper might have been a very slight he, for all that was distinguishable. The person was swathed head to toe in thick black cloth, and dark glasses covered the eyes. Mesh opening allowed for easy breathing where a nose and mouth ought to be.

It took me a moment to make sense of this bizarre getup, but then it came to me. She'd come prepared to face a potentially hostile executioner and her dragon, and she was taking no chances. No bare skin for Bjartur, no eyes for me. They couldn't know how fiercely I protected my own self from others. The last thing I was likely to do was attempt to see someone, anyone, I didn't absolutely have to.

"I'm here for the girl," she hissed quietly, the timbre of her voice further convincing me that she was in fact *she*.

Instinctively I placed myself more solidly between her and the path to Allora, motioning behind myself with my spare arm. I was sure Allora was watching from under the bed, and I didn't want her to come barreling back out. My efforts were useless, as it turned out. Allora was not the most obedient of children.

"I don't know who you are!" I hissed back. "Do you realize there are guards everywhere?"

Somehow the woman managed to cast me a look of utter disdain right through those sunglasses.

"Shift change," she snarled, as if that were supposed to mean something to me. I never paid the least mind to what the guards were doing. "Not that they usually pay much attention, anyway. You're probably the least suspicious person in the entire country."

Really? I wasn't sure how I felt about that. Relieved, was how I *ought* to feel. But what about all the other executioners? Shouldn't any one of us be equally beyond question in our loyalty? Who sacrificed and dedicated our lives to the state more than us? Was it possible I was somehow the most feared of them all?

I nearly snorted in laughter at that thought, tried hastily to swallow it back, and ended up in a coughing fit that sent Bjartur sprawling with a reproachful look in my direction. I straightened up with some difficulty and returned to my first point, trying to ignore the shuffling behind me. The obnoxious child had come right back out of hiding. How she decided this ninja-looking creature posed less risk than the housekeeper, I couldn't begin to fathom

"I don't know you. You're not taking her." By the tautening of her posture, my words surprised her as much as they did me.

"You got our message last night. *They were never your parents, and they're not dead.* Stop stalling and let me get out of here with her while I still can. Your guards may be lax, but they're not unconscious."

I shook my head, crossing my arms. "Where she goes, we go. And I'm guessing you already know the housekeeper will be here any minute now, so make up your mind."

The figure in black shook her head and drew a gun from behind her back. Bjartur had already sensed my directive and landed on

Allora's shoulder. I stepped aside so my visitor could see the child clearly.

"You look well-protected but she is not," I told the woman drily. "Bjartur is much faster than your trigger finger. What risk are you willing to take?"

For a moment no one moved. She had no way of knowing that, for whatever reasons of his own, Bjartur was as likely to strike Allora as to strike me. Finally she relented, reholstering her weapon. "Fine," she said. "But we've wasted enough time. Follow me, and do exactly as I say, when I say it. No questions. No hesitation."

"We should take some food with us," I said, already thinking longingly of the huevos rancheros I'd been planning to make for breakfast. With cheese. So much cheese. "Allora, get your shoes on. Oh, and I need to feed my octopus. And we have to be back by nightfall. I have dragon eggs to care for."

"Then stay here! Once we leave, we aren't coming back. But she comes with me."

Allora sat down. "Morrigan," she said with perfect clarity.

It was just occurring to me that I could barely manage my own rebellious streak, much less hers too, when we all froze at the sound of the front gate opening. The housekeeper was here.

I hoped.

If it wasn't the housekeeper, it was probably Doom calling, and I'd had my fill of unexpected visitors already.

Allora was already scrambling. "Under the bed!" I snapped at my latest unwanted responsibility. "Follow her. In the bedroom."

Bjartur would have been perfectly content to sail into hiding with them, but I called him back irritably. "You belong with me," I scolded when he settled huffily onto the kitchen counter. "Don't you forget it."

As long as we were all stuck here a while, I didn't see the sense in waiting any longer to make breakfast. I pulled eggs, tortillas, onions, peppers, and cheese out onto the butcher block. I tossed a habanero to my dragon, who held it with one claw and nibbled at it as fussily as an English duchess might sip a cup of tea. By the time the house-keeper had knocked on the front door, chorizo was sizzling in the skillet.

Sure enough, this rendition of housekeeper was still female. I had no way of knowing if she was the same one I'd seen the last time I'd been home when she came round or not. What interest did house-keepers hold for me? I waved her through nonchalantly.

"Have a look 'round, but I don't really think there's much needs doing. I have a list of supplies I need, though. And I'll be home all this week, so I think I'll just muddle along by myself till I go back to work next Monday."

She nodded without a trace of suspicion. No reason to question that, after all. I typically sent the housekeeper packing on my days home. She padded quietly away through the house, looking for I don't know what signs of general filth and disarray that might require urgent attention before returning to the kitchen for my list. I'll admit I took a rather mean satisfaction in what had to be that little ninja's heart-pounding anxiety as the housekeeper made up the bed and put out fresh towels in my bathroom. I imagined her eyes bulging behind the dark glasses as the housekeeper's sneakered feet passed within an inch or two of her nose and grinned to myself.

The housekeeper was almost out the door with my list in hand when I called her back. Just to send one more little spear of anxiety shafting through my under-the-bed resident. "Oh, and can you pick up some doughnuts and some more crabs for the octopus?"

"No problem," she said, although even as sheltered as I was from the humdrum rabbiting of normal life, I suspected nothing could be further from the truth. Surely live crabs weren't readily available at the grocery store. But maybe people out there in the world I could only dimly imagine had access to all sorts of resources I knew nothing of. The door closed behind her, and seconds later, I heard the engine of her car quietly rumbling away down the drive.

"All clear!"

Allora and the ninja emerged from the bedroom. It's funny how something as commonplace as dust bunnies clinging to one's balaclava can render a person completely unthreatening. Allora stepped around her and clambered up onto a stool with an expectant look on her face. I shoveled my concoction onto a plate and pushed it toward her.

Whatever part of the world Allora was from, she wasn't accustomed to a bland diet. She didn't even blink at the hot peppers. I filled a saucer with Tabasco, and Bjartur took his place on the counter beside her, slurping discreetly as his jeweled eyes rotated from me to our stranger and back to me again.

The woman bent and drew a long knife from a sheath on her tall black boots. "We need to go, now. This is not a game, and I will do whatever is necessary to complete this extraction."

I took a big bite gooey with cheese and chewed unconcernedly. "You won't kill her, and you can't kill me without Bjartur immediately taking her out, and then what will become of you? You're just going to have to calm down, slow down, and explain what's going on here. First things first. What's your name?"

Allora kept eating as quickly as she could throughout all this. I suspected she'd survived far more tense situations and been more hungry in the process. Bjartur, in spite of his pretended nonchalance, listened closely too, his barbed tail poised for takeoff.

The woman replaced her blade in its sheath with a muttered imprecation and peeled off her balaclava, revealing mussed spiky hair and a pair of black eyes that glinted threateningly at me before she smashed her sunglasses back on. Her skin was about the same shade as Allora's and mine. Through gritted teeth, she said, "Riker."

I filled another plate and motioned to the empty stool on the other side of Bjartur. "Might as well eat, Riker. The next shift change won't be for hours. I'm thinking you missed your window."

Riker snarled. I smiled. "So what is going on here? Who are you with, and what do you want with Allora?"

"You better than anyone know the danger of knowledge. You never wanted to be part of this. Bedelia didn't choose you for your soft heart. She chose you for your utility, which you've now served. Let me take her and leave, and you never have to think about us again."

Logically, I had no reason to argue with her. I didn't want to be part of this. But somehow, I couldn't bring myself to abandon Allora to whatever might wait for her outside my walls. At least if I'd executed her, I'd have known she never suffered for a moment. What if these people wanted to abuse her? To manipulate her so that her powers could be perverted to fit whatever violent cause they espoused? The kid had already endured who knew what privations in her short life. If she stayed with me, I could figure out a way to keep her safe. I could come up with some longer-term solution than a little shelter in the woods. She'd have books and food and Bjartur and Morrigan. Surely that was enough for any child.

Yes. I was basically intending to keep her as a pet. So I threw up a few roadblocks.

"But I am part of this. And she's my responsibility now, whether I like it or not. I'm not going to hand her over to a weird woman dressed all in black who breaks into my home and could easily get me or all of us killed. Reasons."

"Fine. Short version. She's a seer, just like you. The state will brainwash her and turn her into a killer for their machine, just like you. I'm here to stop that from happening. People like me are going to shatter this rotten, corrupt country into a thousand pieces. But till then, you can go back to your pretty little glass cage, keep eating your omelettes and turning your damn dragon eggs, and forget all about us."

My mouth opened and closed uselessly a few times, so I shoved some more tortillas in while I tried to decide what of all that to dissect first.

15

"Long version," I finally said. "We've got all day. And your short version makes absolutely no sense at all."

Riker delayed with some eating of her own but relented in the end. I suspected posturing was important to this one. She needed to make a show of resisting even what she knew to be inevitable. It seemed likely that was a common trait among rebels of all stripes. How else could they persist on paths sure to be dead ends? I'm not a particularly patient person – I've never needed to be, but decades of seeing people can't help but engender a sort of sympathy. Or at least an acknowledgment of what sort of lies different kinds of people need to tell themselves to survive. All people, however honest they imagine themselves, however honest they might even be regarding others, rely on these lies to persist.

I didn't need to see Riker to know what her lies were. People aren't as unique as they like to believe they are. Riker was full of fear and needed to believe she was brave. She was at a loss as to how to deal with Allora and me both, and she needed to believe she had a plan. She was more than a little at my mercy, and she needed to believe she had the upper hand. Perhaps most importantly, she needed to believe she was one of the good guys. Was that one a lie?

I didn't know. I didn't even know if there were any good guys. And me? I definitely wasn't one.

"Start at the beginning," I prompted, willing to play the part of petitioner if it would move her along. "My beginning. What does all this mean about my parents?"

Riker pursed her lips. "Well, the people you're calling your parents weren't. I don't know for sure what happened to your real parents, but they either died trying to reach this country with you or they were killed once they made it. You were probably Allora's age or younger. Much older, and they dispose of dragon-talkers. Too much trouble, too much trauma. Irreparable stuff."

"You're saying my parents – me – I'm an invader?"

"All dragon-talkers are. Dragons and dragon-talkers all come from the same regions of the world. They haven't figured out if it's a genetic thing or some kind of cross-cultural knowledge shared between the two species. Northern Africa, the Middle East, Eastern Europe. There's a few different species of dragons, of course, but the variations are slight."

Bjartur had finished his hot sauce and was watching her closely. Listening.

"Not that there's any dragons left over there now, though. Between your state, the Eastern Empire, and that damned island, you bombed the shit out of every known den once you'd extracted your breeding pairs. The Dragon Proliferation Treaty ensures no dragons left in the wild and no dragons sold to parties unapproved by the Big Three."

Bjartur fluttered over to our little clutch and settled his body gently atop them, draping his wings across the manger like two iridescent leather blankets. He wasn't looking at Riker anymore. His gleaming eyes were fixed on me.

Pain radiated from him, pain but not surprise. Had he known this all along? Did dragons have some sort of collective memory?

Hell, for all I knew, they could communicate with each other, even when separated by distance.

Surely I would have recognized the sort of grief and loss such an event would have prompted in Bjartur. But then, I supposed it had happened before either of us were born. Was genocide still traumatic if you grew up with the knowledge and expectation of it?

This felt very much like an appropriately sweary moment. Sweary and surreal.

I did my best to put all emotions aside, skepticism included, and absorb as much information as I could. Allora, having emptied her plate, slid off her stool and returned to my bedroom, where I was sure she was communing with Morrigan in her tank. I should bathe that kid, I thought absently. That's the sort of thing a caregiver ought to do, on a schedule of some kind.

No wonder dragon-hatching was such a vital part of my job. If what Riker said was true, the powers-that-be had reduced the dragon population to at least threatened, if not endangered, status, and now maintaining that population was entirely their responsibility. Dragons were long-lived, which was a plus, but according to what I'd been taught when training for my imprint, gestations were rare. Dragons are sort of the baobabs of the animal world.

I shook myself free of my musings and fixed what I hoped was an untroubled stare on Riker.

"And I'm not a citizen."

Riker shrugged. "I don't know if the state naturalizes executioners or not. But you definitely weren't born here. No executioners were. The people you thought were your parents had one purpose: to instill you with sufficient empathy and emotional intelligence to be able to effectively use your natural seer abilities. It doesn't always work, apparently. But nobody knows much about what happens to those individuals. That's why they only even try to use the very young. Any older, and they might be too permanently scarred, have too much baggage of their own to survive, you know, becoming a stone-cold killer who knows exactly what they're doing and exactly what they're destroying."

She all but spat the words. It was almost as if she didn't like me. A rather hysterical amusement intruded, and I couldn't resist a chuckle, which didn't endear me to her any further.

"How do they know which invaders have the gift?"

"The same way you found Allora. When an executioner encounters someone they can't see, it's someone with the gift. Like I said, if they're too old, the state has other means of disposal. They figure they're not common enough to worry about a few seer ghosts drifting around. It's not like committing genocide against entire races of people. They've finally learned those costs are too high, so they use freaks like you."

I laughed again. How could I not? She was such a contradictory bundle of hates.

"But you're risking your life alongside people like me, aren't you? You all but admitted other executioners are already actively disloyal to the state. Are they freaks, too?"

She shifted uncomfortably. "They're probably not anyone's favorite people. It's – complicated to make friends with someone who's almost certainly killed people you loved and never lost a minute's sleep over it. But at least the ones with us have changed. They're risking their lives, too. And we need them. We can't do this without them."

I was definitely going to come back to that. But first...

"So, my parents' car crash was faked? The funeral was faked? They just – what? Punched their clock and went back to their normal lives? Were they even actually married to each other?"

Riker shrugged again. "How would I know? I never worked for the state. I'm an invader, too. Well, my parents were invaders. I was born here. Most of what we know is what we've pieced together. Maybe they were married. Maybe they weren't even heterosexual. Who knows? But what they definitely were? State employees doing a job."

In spite of my best efforts at impartial review of her story, I felt nauseous. What sort of people could convince a child they loved her more than anything else in the world, when all along they intended to break her heart and abandon her without a backward glance, *for a paycheck?* What irony. Surely the only people who could raise up a child with extraordinary empathy just so she could be turned into a killing arm of the state were the most perfect sociopaths.

I understood what the words meant, but the reality, if that's what it was, couldn't sink in. I *knew* my parents loved me. I knew I loved them. I'd been there. Riker was spouting what she'd been told by people who hated me, that was all. The bedtime stories, the trips to the park, the after-dinner board games, the way my dad would chuck my chin, the look in my mom's eyes when I was sick: those were all real. This preposterous story told by a confessed rebel and invader was nonsense.

I ignored my churning stomach and pushed on. What other madness did she believe? What madness was she capable of committing?

"So what is this grand plan you've got? I fail to see how a handful of fugitive invaders and some turncoat executioners could hope to overturn a perfectly successful state."

She snorted. "You have no idea what the state is or isn't." She gestured to my room. "No phone, no television, no computer, no radio, right? All you know is what you're told. And I'm definitely not telling you anything about our plans. All you need to know is that we are the ones who will actually keep Allora safe instead of turning her into someone like you."

Bjartur left our clutch and soared over to my lap, curling into a circle of purring warmth. Love and strength poured into my body with his rumbles. I clung to that sensation like a lifeline. This, the love of my dragon, at least, I knew incontrovertibly to be true and real.

"Maybe you haven't noticed, but I have a pretty good life. A beautiful home, on a beautiful estate, the housekeeper gets me whatever I want. Bjartur and I have a bond you could never understand. I get to raise dragon eggs. I'm never hungry or cold or worried about where I'm going to sleep at night. I'm not afraid of anything. The life you're offering Allora is one of constant uncertainty and danger. And it definitely lacks my amenities."

"You'd really sentence another child to what you went through? All memory of the parents who sacrificed everything in the desperate hope you'd survive erased, fake parents and fake trauma forced on you, years of training and brainwashing after that, and then a lifetime of killing innocent people?"

"I don't kill innocent people. The people I execute have all been fairly sentenced by the state."

"Yeah, sentenced for the crime of trying to live. Do you know how bad things are over there? Drought and famine and an endless series of wars have left that part of the world little better than a scarred husk. It can't support a population. People do not throw their children into an inflatable raft to cross an ocean if they have any other option at all for survival."

"I don't know anything about all that. I know it's illegal to invade our shores and attempt to access our resources without proper authorization, and executing people who commit illegal acts is my job. I'm not a monster. They don't suffer. It might be the only time in their entire life anyone has actually seen them, and Bjartur is the most merciful of creatures. It's hardly a despicable act."

Riker stared at me, speechless. She shook her head slowly.

"They weren't kidding. You really are above suspicion, aren't you? Mostly because you're too oblivious to be suspicious of anything yourself. You do realize that just by helping Allora as much as you have, you've already earned yourself one of your own 'fairly sentenced' executions, don't you?"

Now that struck home. I did indeed realize that and had spent no small amount of time considering it. But the fact that I didn't want to die didn't mean that killing me was inherently unjust, did it? Not wanting to die was part of the natural human state. Needing to die was, too. Everything else was just timing and logistics.

"I mean, in for a penny, in for a pound, right?" she persisted. I had to give it to her, distasteful as she might find me, she was determined to win me over all the same. "You're already worthy of death by your own standards. For nothing more than giving a child a couple extra days of life. If anyone finds out, you'll never convince them you aren't one of us. You might as well throw in with us and try to make it all mean something."

"Dying for a lost cause I don't believe in doesn't sound more meaningful than dying because some office drone tricked me. Besides, there's one more thing bothering me. Your little organization seems to be going to a lot of lengths to secure as many seers as they can, be they children or executioners. And you've made it clear that's not out of the goodness of your heart. You said they're part of your plan. So I fail to see how you are any better than the state. They want to use us for something, so do you. Either way, Allora is a pawn."

Riker sucked her lips but said nothing.

"It seems to me that her best life is here with me and Bjartur and Morrigan. And you already know she agrees, if that's worth anything at all. It might be a little tricky, but at least she has a chance to be a child instead of a tool."

The words bamboozled me more than they did Riker, though I tried to keep my expression placidly smug. *What am I doing?* If these people were willing to take Allora off my hands and leave me to my peaceful existence, all reason dictated I should let them. Now I was proposing I should keep her indefinitely?

Yup. That was what I was doing. Bjartur's humming increased, a sure sign of his approval.

16

I shifted Bjartur into my arms and left Riker at the kitchen bar. Going into my own bedroom in my own house wasn't hiding. I was checking on my charge, like a responsible person. Sure enough, Allora sat on her knees in front of Morrigan's tank, a hand pressed on the glass. Morrigan had one tentacle against the glass on her side, and she looked for all the world as if she were intently listening to the earnest thoughts Allora was clearly pouring in her direction.

For lack of anything better to do, I sank onto the floor beside her and settled Bjartur back onto my lap. He grunted an unconvincing rebuke but quickly resumed purring. Allora ducked her chin and slid her eyes in my direction, immediately returning her attention to the octopus.

The tank was enormous, and already I found myself fretting it was too small. How big was an octopus' territory when in the wild? Suddenly I was consumed with guilt. I didn't want Morrigan to be bored or feel trapped. I would need to change things in her tank frequently so she'd feel as if she had new territory to explore. Should I get some other sort of sea creature, a companion? Did octopuses make friends with other animals? I knew better than to keep an animal in a cage. *I knew better.* But was that the same thing I was attempting to do with Allora? And if keeping an octopus alive was complicated, how much more difficult would it be to keep Allora? A child needed more resources to grow than a few fake rocks and a handful of crabs.

I swallowed a hysterical giggle. How exactly did I think I was going to accomplish any of this? I had no way of knowing what was happening now at the Justice Center. At any moment, the soldiers guarding my gate might be directed to bring me in to face my own swift trial and execution. On the slim chance that suspicion left me unscathed, what would the Center be like when I returned? Would Fiske still be there? Would I have to execute him like I'd had to execute Shovel? Would I get a new Shovel who could supply Bjartur and me with everything we needed, like had always happened before when an assistant was replaced, or would there be some massive restructuring?

What nonsense to think I could take on a child when my own life was in such upheaval.

Still, I found my gaze drawn to Allora's curls that sprang so carelessly, her soft fat cheeks that glowed with the same burnished hue as my own. We were alike, weren't we? Maybe everything else Riker had said had been some sort of outrageous propaganda, but this was undeniable. For all our differences, we were two of a kind.

She a child, me a woman approaching old age. Both of us orphans. Our spoken languages were not the same, but she seemed to communicate effortlessly with Bjartur and Morrigan without the clumsy construction of words. And it did seem we shared the same gift for seeing, even if hers had not yet been pupiled. Her fate lay in my hands, at least partially, and in a strange way, mine lay in hers.

How had I gone from such perfect contentment to this mangled disaster of a dilemma?

Allora sat back and crossed her legs, opening her arms in an invitation for Bjartur to abandon me, which of course he accepted. I returned my attention to the octopus, who had drifted away from the glass and seemed to be practicing her chameleon skills along the bottom of the tank. For the thousandth time, I heard Magenna's words echoing in my head.

"You still don't understand anything about octopuses, do you?"

It wasn't as if I believed witches actually possessed any magical abilities. Everything in my life had taught me that magic was a myth. From what I gathered, the most threatening thing about witches was their knowledge of natural medicines. The state had long since dispensed with the luxury of accommodating or extending the lives of people who offered return value inconsistent with the effort of keeping them alive. Disabilities of any kind, chronic illnesses, and dangerous viruses were short-lived, because so were the people who had them. Witches posed a serious threat to the system by supplying two commodities the state outlawed: remedies and hope.

I didn't know much, if anything, about the situation Riker had been talking about on the European and African continents, but I did know resource management was one of our state's great success stories. Due in no small measure to the fact that we didn't waste any of it on people who could only drain the system. It wasn't the most comfortable or cheery thing to think about, but I had no philosophical argument with which to counter it. A society needed every member to contribute, to participate, to at least carry their own weight and then to support the weight of the state as well. Otherwise, while it might take decades or even centuries, eventually the society would be swallowed up by its own hunger. Simple math, wasn't it?

Witches like Magenna must use a different equation than the ones I knew to justify their choices. It baffled me that many of them actually came from these invader countries, where they'd seen first-hand the suffering that resulted when the number of mouths outstripped the seats at the table. They risked their lives getting to our borders in all sorts of impossibly perilous ways, but then insisted on repeating here the same mistakes that had doomed them to that fate there. Surely they could see how much healthier a society was when purged of its weak and its ailing.

However perplexing her personal choices, though, the Magenna I'd seen was not the sort to throw away her last words. Maybe it hadn't been a last communication so much as a last manipulation. I had to own it a fully successful one, at that. I'd gotten an octopus, hadn't I? And spent countless hours drifting in contemplation of what octopuses contemplated, what witches contemplated. Could Magenna's meaning have been as simple and petty as that? Or had she been trying to tell me something she truly thought would serve me later, something I was no closer to comprehending now than I had been on the day I executed her?

Morrigan shifted, sand-colored, along the bed of her tank. I relented, relaxed, retreated. Dropped my walls, so she could come in. If she chose.

She chose.

Ripples of sensation undulated not over but through every cell. Words could no longer frame or contain any meaning. Color and light sieved through my consciousness. Music hummed through my body, and later I would realize that was only all the thousand waves of ambient sound symphonying along my veins instead of banging dully on my eardrums. Life thrummed along every tentacle, every sucker, every particle, finding no limit in thought or pain or hunger or a heartbeat. Powerful. Playful. Capricious. Curious.

Curious. That gentle stroke of something like a question at the door of my own, locked-away self brought me back into my body, but the loss of connection was a tricky business, like peeling away a leech. Morrigan was all suckers, wasn't she? Whatever sentience she possessed was not only self-aware but other-aware, too. What a strange little alien being she was. Amazing to think the ocean was teeming with mysteries just like her: singular, self-possessed creatures who wondered and learned and explored, just like we do, but with whom we have never compared sagas or chronicles. Creatures we fry up and eat rather than listen to and learn from. Such a poverty, our plenty.

Morrigan was floating now, having shed the color of sand for something nearer the purple hue of her aquarium light. Her tentacles ribboned in my direction, and she was gone, propelled into her favorite den among the rocks.

Enough woolgathering. It couldn't be a good idea to leave Riker unattended for long, even if I doubted her ability to cause too much trouble without attracting the attention of the guards, which was clearly a major deterrent for her. I tugged Allora to her feet, ignoring the reproachful looks she and Bjartur alike cast me for disturbing his happy nap, and we returned to the living room where Riker paced like a restless black jaguar.

I shouldn't have been surprised that I underestimated her. Given my very limited experience with underworld characters in general, I was bound to underestimate anyone. Still, it did come as a terrible shock when my error finally dawned on me.

We'd successfully managed the housekeeper's return visit without rousing the slightest suspicion, and I was ruminating about dinner when Riker outfoxed me.

"We have five minutes," she said grimly behind me. I turned around to see her holding one of my precious dragon eggs under her arm. I swallowed air, choking. Bjartur let out a caterwaul that would have raised goosebumps on a ghost. He flapped around her head and shoulders, and I called him to me desperately, terrified he would startle her into dropping her burden.

Dragon eggs aren't as thin-shelled as robin eggs or goose eggs, but there was little hope of it surviving if it was dropped. Even if by some miracle it didn't crack, the trauma would surely kill the infant inside. Bjartur hesitated but finally came to me, his talons gripping my shoulder fearfully even as he kept his wings outstretched in the most intimidating posture he could muster. Low growls rolled ceaselessly from his throat.

"What are you doing? You have no idea how delicate those are. Put it back!"

"I have plenty of an idea how delicate they are. Delicate enough to persuade you to do what I say in order to protect it. If you try to use that dragon against me or against Allora, I'll smash it on the ground. Try me."

Terror coursed through my body. I hadn't felt true fear in so long, it had the oddest impact of both horror and exhilaration hitting me at once with the same punch in the gut. I felt light-headed. Even when Shovel had compromised me and I realized I might be next in line for execution, I hadn't felt this kind of fear. That worry had possessed the quality of the hypothetical, the luxury of the possible.

My dragon egg was real, present. A baby I'd been nurturing and protecting and dreaming over for months, years. And in less time than it would take me to yell, this complete stranger might kill it. Unexpectedly, tears filled my eyes.

"Don't," I begged. "Please don't. I'll do whatever you say. Just – be careful. There's a baby dragon in there. You'll hurt it."

Riker flashed me a blinding smile before yanking her balaclava over her face. "I won't hurt it at all. I'll *end* it. Now, if you ever want to get this precious egg back in your nasty hands, you'd better follow me and do exactly as I say."

"What about the housekeeper? What if she comes back and finds me gone?"

Riker shrugged. "What, like you never take a walk? Not that I buy the idea she's going to come out here three times in one day. And frankly, once we get off this compound, I really don't care. What becomes of you isn't part of my purview. What becomes of her, is."

At Riker's nod in her direction, Allora scrambled across the room and huddled behind me. I could feel the tension radiating through her scrawny body as she wrapped both hands around my forearm and stood ramrod straight.

"Fine. Whatever you say. Tell us what to do."

"Through the back door. Run as fast as you can for the woods. We have a few minutes while the guards shuffle around at the gate."

I didn't hesitate. I grabbed Allora's hand and took off out the back door like the hounds of hell were after us. Bjartur lifted off my shoulder as soon as we were clear of the house, flying low and swiftly ahead of us like a dark, iridescent arrow guiding our way. I didn't look back, but I had no doubt that demon woman was on my tail. I only prayed she didn't stumble with my baby in her arms.

I didn't allow myself to think about the other two eggs left behind. Dragons were social creatures, all the way down to the biological level. Just as they were aware of Bjartur and me and craved our voices and our presence, they were aware of each other, too. These three eggs had never been apart from one another since they arrived. I didn't know what sort of trauma a sudden separation might induce, and right now I didn't have time to worry about it. If I could keep this one egg from being destroyed, I'd count it as a win. Finding my way back and restoring it to its clutch was a whole other problem I couldn't solve right now. I couldn't afford to think past one catastrophe at a time.

By the time we pounded into the shelter of the trees, my chest was burning and my side felt like someone had driven a steak knife through it. Bjartur sat on the branch of an elm, his eyes burning with hate like I'd never seen. Allora skidded to a halt and spun around, her gaze, like mine, going immediately to the glowing egg still tucked securely under Riker's arm.

"Keep going," Riker ordered shortly. "Fall in behind me. Unless they have some reason to review the footage, no-one should be looking for us, but we can't be sure."

"Can I hold the egg, please?"

"What sort of idiot do you take me for? Of course you can't hold the egg."

Allora slipped a sweaty hand into mine, for all the world as if she were comforting me. Little upstart. But I squeezed back and held on, anyway. Bjartur couldn't rest. He rode on my shoulder, rode on Allora's shoulder, fluttered alongside Riker, always with his eyes on the egg. It wasn't his egg, of course, not exactly, but he and I both felt as if all the eggs who came into our home *were* ours. We celebrated all their little milestones and dreaded the day when they'd be taken from us on the eve of their hatch and imprint. We mourned them when they left, knowing already the little personalities and quirks that were just on the cusp of blossoming within those colorful shells. We tried not to wonder where they went or who they became far away from us, but we never forgot them.

Riker had seized on the one thing that would ensure our cooperation, that was true, but she had no idea the enemy she'd created in my fierce little dragon. I did not have high hopes for her long life after this. Nor did I care.

17

Riker was communicating with someone or some*ones*, speaking into a small device she'd had tucked in a pocket. A walkie-talkie or a radio was my best guess. We tramped through the forest for what felt like hours, pushing through brambles and wild rose bushes and ducking under branches. I thought perhaps I'd wandered this far when I was young, when I'd first been assigned here, but I couldn't be sure. I wasn't exactly an outdoorsy type, so while I appreciated the forest for the protection it gave me and the hunting ground it afforded Bjartur, I'd felt no compulsion to spend hours in the muggy Southern summers exploring it. It was pretty, it was green, it was there. I'd always been perfectly content with my air conditioning and my board games and my books.

So I had no real idea of where we were or how far we'd traveled by the time we finally reached the wall that marked the edge of my domain. It was constructed of some sort of metal sheeting and stood about twelve feet tall. It was almost entirely obscured by the forest that surrounded it, so it didn't appear until we'd walked nearly right up on it.

I was not impressed. Surely anyone with more arboreal talents than me could simply climb the trees high enough to get themselves over.

Or, as Riker demonstrated after kicking aside a pile of leaves and brush to lift a wooden door, dig a tunnel to go underneath.

I wondered, as I had been increasingly these past few days, if these defenses were built to protect me or to contain me. I pushed the question aside and scrambled into the dank, timber-framed corridor at the jerk of Riker's head. Once inside, I turned back to help Allora down.

I could see from the look on her face she wasn't thrilled at the notion of stepping down into an underground pit of darkness, but she only sucked in her lips and held tightly to my hand as she followed me in. Bjartur, on the other hand, simply soared over the fence. Lucky beastie. I hoped this tunnel was short enough that we wouldn't get separated.

Riker came last, clicking on a flashlight she wore clipped to her belt and shining it ahead of me as she pulled the door closed over her head. Happily our subterranean trek only lasted a few yards before I reached another wooden ladder that led to a door back into the dim forest daylight. Bjartur was perched on a branch waiting for us, one talon clicking impatiently against the bark. I glanced along the fencing, wondering if there were cameras out here, too, and where they might be pointed. Riker seemed unconcerned about the possibility of being observed now, though, so I assumed any surveillance had been dealt with one way or another.

Riker took the lead again, moving decisively through the tangle of trees and underbrush. All I could do was follow with my eyes glued to the dragon egg, breath bated for fear she'd trip over a root or lose her footing in a gopher hole and crush her precious freight. Bjartur had settled back on my shoulders, his claws digging anxiously into my skin through the flannel shirt.

Without warning, the woods opened up, and we were standing on the edge of a narrow dirt road. Three men stood beside a nondescript station wagon-type vehicle some shade of grey or blue or silver, spotted with rust. Wearing bulky jackets, ballcaps, and sunglasses, they might as well have been invisible for all the identifying characteristics they offered. I couldn't even be sure of the shade of their skin. Allora grabbed my forearm with both hands and huddled close, coming to a dead stop.

That's when I spotted the dart-shaped crimson head resting on one of those black-clad shoulders, silver eyes gleaming. That's when I felt such unutterable, urgent, hopeless, hopeful, aching yearning from the creature on my shoulder that tears filled my eyes and poured down my cheeks with no way at all to stop them. I stopped, too, choking on sobs not my own and freeing my arm just enough to pull Allora closer still.

And even then, Bjartur waited. I did not need to guess what waiting cost him: I could feel it in my bones, in my veins, in my every cell. But he waited, conscious of the egg Riker carried, conscious of the danger around us all. Nonetheless he was completely unafraid of his fellow dragon, whose eyes clung as desperately to Bjartur as Bjartur's clung to him.

Slowly my mind asserted its own presence, winning back its thoughts from Bjartur's overwhelming emotions. If that creature was a dragon, then that man was a seer. And if that man was a seer, then it was hardly possible he could be anything other than another executioner, one who had somehow wrung himself free of the shackles of the state and joined this bizarre rebellion.

Bjartur ached for his fellow. And I, mysteriously, unexpectedly, ached for mine.

Here was someone who had walked my same path. Someone who carried my same burdens, my same weights. Who practiced my same dark and unforgiving art. Someone who knew life and death more intimately than anyone else I'd ever met, besides myself.

And he was standing not as my ally but as my enemy. Rationally I processed this, but my heart protested that no stranger whom I knew so well could truly be a foe. I stepped forward, opening my inner eye, straining to see this mirror of myself.

But just as had happened with Allora, I saw nothing at all.

I shook my head against the odd sensation of banging into a wall. The man and his dragon hadn't moved at all.

"What's with the egg?" asked the stoutest of the three.

"Persuasion," Riker said grimly.

At the sound of her voice, my brain finally started clacking along its track again. Somehow I had to persuade these mad people to let me go back home with both my egg and Allora. I had nothing with which to tempt or threaten them. No bargaining chips. In desperation, I dropped my walls and looked in at each of them, consequences be damned. All my years of prudence would mean nothing if, in this moment, with these people, I couldn't find a way to save what I loved,

Sal, the stout one. A murky swamp crawling with alligators and leeches, where ebullient flowers gasped out heady fragrance and dragonflies dart dazzling in the sun. A soul determined to reach the still warmth islanded in the dark and treacherous water, a soul undeterred by whatever slime and muck might cling to his skin in the attempt.

Lester. Paper-white peeling bark, golden eyes peering out from a multitude of slender stretching trunks on a mountain slope. An aspen's grace and idealism matched only by its indomitable survival, its adventitious roots sending out innumerable clones and clasping hands close in even the shallowest, ash-riven soil. A believer in sunshine and the inevitability of life.

Great. A couple of true believers and an executioner whom I didn't doubt to be as practical and cold-eyed as myself. Not the easiest sorts to sway.

On my shoulder, Bjartur shifted foot to foot. At any moment I might lose him. His want was growing louder and his will weaker.

"May they meet?" I asked, gesturing to the stranger's dragon. He tipped his head, ever so slightly, and both dragons soared from their perches to the dusty, leaf-littered ground. They held their wings stiffly, like cormorants drying in the sun, and walked in ginger circles, first this way, then that, their heads cocked and their eyes inquisitive. Soon they began talking to each other, in low hums, high-pitched whistles, and scaling trills.

It was a fearful and wonderful sight, and something in me nearly cracked to see it. I've read that people are stronger at the broken places once they heal, but I've found it to be even more true that real strength comes from resisting the break in the first place. It's one thing to empathize with someone. It's something else entirely, something I can't afford, to let their pain split your own heart in two. That way lies madness, at least for an executioner. How other people survive, I have no idea.

But Bjartur wasn't some random other. He was the closest thing I could imagine to a soulmate. A being who simply existed with me. Who accepted everything about me, who stood beside me on every field, who shared my mind and heart and intentions. Who didn't demand a justification for what we did but only the expectation that we would do it together. Whose purrs and hums and snores and songs bounded all my hours.

And in that moment, I stood awash in the ache that blindsided him, in the longing, in the sudden, unforeseen loneliness that swallowed him.

Loneliness?

Fear came trampling in then, all my own. If Bjartur was lonely for another dragon, for other dragons, how could I ever hold him again? Likely this was one reason the state kept dragons separated from one another from the moment they hatched. In the wild, they were communal creatures, nothing like the solitary monsters of myth. What had I done by bringing him here? My heart pounded furiously. I was torn between calling Bjartur back and the horrifying possibility that he might ignore me.

The other seer spoke. "My name is Finnick," he said. "This is Varg."

"Grenda," I responded slowly. "And Bjartur."

The two dragons had dropped their wings and were rubbing

their cheeks along each other's necks, humming loudly in their discordant voices. I tried to keep my growing alarm out of my face.

"You didn't bring much with you."

"We're not staying," I said flatly. "Riker has my arm twisted at the moment, but we aren't joining your merry band."

I suspect this part of the story will disappoint you. I was disappointed, too, but this is no fairytale. In real life, tough choices have to be made all the time, and there's no built-in subplot to rob those choices of their less-than-pleasant consequences. Nobody knows hard choices better than an executioner. So brace yourself. I've never been a hero. Just the deadliest of bureaucrats.

Finnick's brows quirked, and something dangerous shifted under his skin, though he didn't move at all. Lester and Sal both tensed and took up positions on either side of me. Riker only stared at me, her eyes flat and amused. She rolled the dragon egg back and forth between her palms. Hatred, unfamiliar and intoxicating, swelled within me.

I heard a musical sigh that might have been a sob from Bjartur. Without so much as a gesture from me, he extracted himself from Varg's embrace and fluttered back to my shoulder. I shuddered with relief as I felt his mind bump back into mine. Allora clutched my hand more tightly, but I peeled her fingers away.

"You'd rather go back to having your every move controlled by a state who stole you from your parents and raised you like an animal to serve their needs?" Finnick's soft voice betrayed none of the outrage of his words.

I shrugged. One of the key benefits of my particular upbringing is a virtual immunity to peer pressure of any sort. "Bjartur and I live very happily together. We have books and cheese and peppers and warm soft blankets. Seems like an obvious advantage over hiding out in the woods, waiting to be caught and executed. Besides, I have eggs to raise."

Finnick gestured to Varg, who'd likewise returned to his shoulder. "I know you can feel the connection between them. Don't you feel any guilt over raising more dragons to be kept isolated from each other like they were? Dragons were never meant to be alone. Just like people. It's a special kind of hell, what our government does, forcing creatures who naturally yearn for each other to live for decades apart from each other just so they can control them. Control us."

Bjartur shifted foot to foot, and those black fingers of fear clutched my heart more tightly. "Bjartur and I aren't alone. We have each other. And until you people interfered with our lives, we were both perfectly content. My baby dragons will have their own imprints who love them the same as I love Bjartur. The only suffering is the sort you create. The kind that results in invaders dying either at sea or in my execution room, in the torments suffered by the sick, in the fear of children like Allora who would have been perfectly cared for if you hadn't intervened. Now her life is probably as forfeit as the rest of yours."

Finnick stared at me for a long moment. He might not be able to see into me, but he took my measure all the same. He turned to the others, dismissing me.

"There's no point arguing with her. She's staying behind."

Sal's hand slid toward his belt, but Lester shook his head. "We don't need to kill her. Anything she might say to betray us spells her own end, and she knows it. The only chance she had with the state might – *might* – have been when Bedelia first sent Allora home with her. Not turning her in right away sealed her own death warrant. She won't say anything."

Riker nodded slowly, her lips curving with satisfaction. "And who knows when we might have need of someone on the inside who's already compromised? And about whose personal safety we really don't give a shit?"

I wasted a glare in her direction. She didn't so much as glance my way.

I wanted my egg back. Now.

"Give me the egg," I said.

Riker smiled. "Then give us Allora."

"You can have her. She'd only get me killed if I tried to keep her anyway. I should have let you have her when you first showed up." I honestly didn't know why I'd fought so hard to resist this outcome. I should have known it was inevitable. But something in me hadn't been able to accept it until now—until this new horrifying possibility that Bjartur might choose another dragon over me emerged. Now all I wanted was to get home, with my dragon and my eggs, and bury my head under my pillows.

Allora had been looking back and forth between us, catching who-knows-how-much of our interchange. Now she simply sat down on my foot and wrapped her arms and legs around my calf. Riker narrowed her eyes at me.

"Yeah, you should have. But you didn't. Why not?" She turned back to Lester. "Maybe she came out here to gather more intelligence to trade on. Maybe she's been working for them all along, and that's why Bedelia's plan worked. Maybe she was supposed to come out here and find out as much as she could before reporting back. I say we kill her to be safe."

Bjarur screeched out defiantly, spreading his wings as wide as he could. Varg responded immediately, matching Bjartur fury for fury, their former camaraderie vanished as if it had never been. Those black fingers eased, and I smiled in spite of everything. The dragons might only be posturing – the creatures could never be compelled to attack each other – but the message was plain. Bjartur was with me.

Finnick came unexpectedly to my defense – sort of.

"She's not worth the bloodshed. Remember, every death comes with a penalty. And she's what she seems to be – cold and selfish. Allora might have been something of a novelty to her, given how empty and predictable her life is, but she's not going to risk its comforts for the sake of a strange child. Not even another seer."

His words stung, but I couldn't argue the point. He was right. I had gotten attached to Allora, like I imagined people got attached to strays who landed on their doorstep, and for a moment there, I'd even considered doing something mad and reckless to keep her out of the clutches of these crazy revolutionaries. But seeing Bjartur with Varg had changed that.

Every step I took nearer to these people and their cause was a step closer to losing Bjartur. Who knew how many dragons shared their company? If Bjartur had reacted so strongly to one other dragon, how long could I hope to hold him if we encountered a whole tribe? Let them think me cold and selfish. I might be cold and selfish, but I was alive, and with Bjartur. What else really mattered beside that?

Riker's mouth twisted, and she shrugged, looking to Sal, who was clearly the one in charge. Riker was undoubtedly deadlier, but he was cooler. After a long moment, he nodded.

"You would know," he conceded to Finnick, and some part of my brain filed away that faintest hint of contempt underlying the words. So even here, among their supposed comrades, executioners remained on the outside. Hardly an incentive to join their little club.

Riker crossed the few yards separating us with a bravado that couldn't hide her uneasiness about the dragon still displaying braggadocio on my shoulder. I took the egg from her, feeling its anxious thrumming in my fingers and tucking it close against my body for heat. "Don't get caught," she said, the words a taunt rather than a warning.

I don't much like remembering the next few minutes. Ending a story with a dragon's swift bite or turning down the political aspirations of strangers cost me nothing, but genuine suffering, however incomprehensible, was nigh on unbearable. All the more reason for seers like me to keep our solitude sacred.

Finnick was the one to stride forward and peel Allora off my leg. Even the presence of Varg couldn't tempt her away. Why or how she'd connected with Bjartur and me and resisted them, I had no understanding. What hurt most was the painful, torturous silence of her sobs.

Children aren't known for their impulse control. It takes an unfathomable amount of fear and trauma for a child to choke on their own agony and grief rather than risk discovery. It was like watching the paroxysms of someone whose mouth has been stitched shut, only she'd wielded the needle herself. And oh, her eyes.

I can still see them even now, if I'm not careful. Accusation and condemnation. And inexplicably, betrayal. As if I had given her any reason to believe I was a safe place. A safe person.

Whatever she imagined she'd seen in me, I hadn't shown her. The lies she'd believed had all been the ones she'd told herself.

So why did I feel so sick, so empty, inside?

I cradled our egg closer and turned away, her every gasp rasping against my skin like angry wild rosebushes, tearing me open and slowing my retreat. But still I retreated.

"Ana!" I heard Finnick shout behind me. I paused, bewildered. Strangely suspended by the unfamiliar syllables. Against my better judgment, I looked back.

He held Allora clasped tightly against his chest now, and Varg lay on Allora's back, wings outstretched as if he shielded her from my gaze.

"Your name," he said. "You weren't always Grenda. The name your parents gave you was Ana."

I shook my head, growling, and plunged on through the woods, back to the safety of home and hearth and manger and tank. Back to my cage

18

There was nothing strange about Bjartur and I traipsing around the property, so getting caught, as Riker put it, was no worry of ours. I felt immeasurably old as I trudged under the trees and across the meadow up the hill to the house, though—as if the weight of a hundred unlived lives lay on my back. Bjartur drifted overhead in lazy circles, never venturing far from the egg I carried so carefully in my arms. I envied his weightless grace.

The egg hummed against my ribs, its colors ribboning ceaselessly over the surface. I didn't like the anxiety I felt emanating from the dragon baby, not one bit. My title with the state and undoubtedly in the minds of the populace was simply executioner, but it would have been much more accurate to name me dragon-keeper. Caring for the infants was the singular obsession of my existence, and I knew Bjartur felt the same. Sadness streamed from him like an invisible wake, but there was no resentment, no hesitation in our decision to return here. He, like me, would have sacrificed anything to keep our eggs safe. *Had* sacrificed everything, I supposed. Everything but me.

We still had each other, and that would have to be enough. Something in me turned grey at the thought that Bjartur would never again be truly happy with me. Never be unencumbered by the knowledge of what he'd given up. From today for the rest of our lives, I'd be the person he'd settled for as part of an impossible compromise.

I shied away from the stillness of the house as I closed the door behind me. All told, Allora had shared this space with us for a matter of hours compared to the decades I'd spent in contented person-less-ness. Her absence shouldn't register as a loss, but somehow, it did. I hurried across the silence and tucked my precious bundle into the manger between the other two eggs, fluffing and arranging the straw warmly around them all.

The eggs that had been left behind glowed brightly at the return of their nest-mate, their tuneless humming hitting a fever pitch as they welcomed the unwilling renegade back into refuge. I heaved a sigh of relief to see all three of them shimmering with what seemed to be equal energy. Perhaps no harm would follow after all.

Bjartur settled in, stretching out his neck between two of the eggs and draping his glittering wings around them all. His eyes closed to slits, and rumbling purrs emanated from his round little belly. My heart swelled, and I blinked back unexpected tears. The little tableau looked so familiar, yet it had been irreversibly altered.

A strange dread plucked at my veins as I walked into my bedroom. I recognized it as reluctance to face Morrigan without the child who had championed her so unreservedly, and grimly I pushed it away. What did octopuses know of this life, after all?

My little adventure had only lasted a few hours, less time than I normally spent away at work. Perhaps Morrigan had not even registered our absence.

The room was dark, scarcely illuminated by the dim purple light gleaming from the octopus tank. I crossed and sank cross-legged to the floor like a penitent at the altar. A few moments of quiet passed, bracketed by the quiet humming of the tank's motor, and then my priest emerged, drifting like seaweed toward me. I pressed my palm on the glass.

I named her Morrigan, but I didn't really know if she was a she or a he. If her captivity was impeding her imperative to mother a horde of little octopus eggs, far more innumerable than any number of dragon clutches I might shepherd, or the imperative to impregnate and then perish. But I could be sure I was interfering with the purpose nature intended for her. Whether that was a great injustice or an unanticipated freedom, I had no way of knowing.

How did octopuses measure a good day? Everything I'd read about them was paradoxical. In nature they were solitary, but in captivity they were highly social, enjoying games and play. Clever and quick-witted, they were masters of disguise who reveled in outwitting captors and foiling cages and locks. They'd been known to explore by night and return innocently to their enclosures by day. So were they lonely out there in the great sea? Did they recognize in us an otherness they could name their own?

Unlike the elephants or the whales, their lives were so wretchedly short. Astonishingly intelligent, they learned at a mad pace for a few short months then died, still alone, having shared none of their knowledge with anyone. Fathers gave up on life once they'd mated, starving to death adrift on deep sea currents. Mothers sacrificed everything to keep constant watch over their clutches of hundreds of eggs, keeping them breathing safely as they moved the water continually over their tiny forms, then perished as their offspring hatched and swam away without a backward glance.

Morrigan would never meet those fates. My prisoner, she was kept from her destiny and from her curse. Did one outweigh the other? I hoped so.

I watched colors shimmer over her skin and wondered if she spoke in hues.

She floated away.

Did she notice Allora's absence? The child had spent an inordinate amount of time in communion with the sea-beastie. Still, in all it was the companionship of only a couple of days.

I shook off the question and pushed away from the tank. A

shower was in order – I wasn't much one for outdoor exertion at the best of times, and I'd been stress-sweating all through the trees as I anxiously shadowed my purloined egg. Not to mention who knew what twigs and insects were tangled in the wiry curls of my hair. Picking out that mess was the least I should accomplish before falling into bed.

But plucking through my unruly hair only reminded me of doing the same for Allora. I'd found her every bit as not-self as I did all other people I encountered in life when we met. A superficial physical resemblance, a tricksy coincidence of skin shades and hair coils, meant little to me. The creature in the world I most recognized myself in was a rather feline male reptile covered in iridescent scales. A fluke of appearance won no kinship from me.

Something had changed during our brief sojourn, though. Oddly enough, in spite of my not being able to see her, or maybe because I couldn't see her, she'd wormed her way into my thinking. Not being able to carry her soul made me more conscious of the perilous fragility of her scaffolding of bones and skin. For the first time in my life since my parents had died, I felt connected to another human being in a more than theoretical fashion. Bound up, somehow. Tangled. As if what happened to Allora didn't just matter to me, it would indelibly change me.

But I was no octopus. I had no intention of giving my life to push someone else a few months further than me into the cycle of life with no better assurance than blind hope that they wouldn't just be eaten by an eel the moment they hit the current. Hope, faith, selflessness, all these so-called virtues were nothing more than rather unconvincing literary devices to my way of thinking.

Still, I hurt. And I wanted to stop hurting.

The invaders were right. Finnick was right. I was no threat to them. I wasn't about to throw away my entire existence to save a child whose life promised to hold all the persistence of a soap bubble. I had dragon eggs and an octopus to see to, books to read, puzzles to finish, fires to stoke when autumn returned and the nights got cool.

All of which might already be in peril. This time away from the office, away from Fiske, away from any sort of situational feedback, had me antsy. It wasn't unusual for Fiske to tell me my services wouldn't be needed for a short time – executions aren't ordered on some kind of regular schedule, after all – but it was very unusual for me to be harboring a fugitive when he told me as much. It was definitely highly unusual for a close member of the upper circles of the Justice Center to be outed as a traitor and executed like Bedelia had been. So maybe I couldn't afford to pretend that simple silence would assure me my own survival.

And what would become of Bjartur if I were executed? Would the state simply reassign him, or would they consider him complicit and execute him, too? In my experience, those without the gift of seeing, those for whom dragons were merely a horrifying and fascinating tool of the state, mostly saw dragons as dumb if dangerous beasts who acted entirely at the behest of their keepers.

There was little concept of the infrangible mental bond between dragons and seers. People tended to think of themselves as so superior to other animals that any sort of peership was unimaginable. From the outside looking in, seers were no more dependent on dragons than a lion-tamer was dependent on a lion or a wetsuit-clad grandstander was dependent on the whales and dolphins she manipulated into playing for the crowds. Perhaps that ignorance would be Bjartur's salvation, if anything happened to me. Being underestimated wasn't always a bad thing.

I didn't sleep in my bed that night. I dragged my covers and pillows onto the floor at the foot of the bed and slept in a pool of Morrigan's violet light, the soundtrack of my dreams the humming of her tank and the snoring of my dragon from the living room. When I woke the next morning, I had a new plan.

19

As masterful plans went, it wasn't very impressive. I had pitifully little to work with. Fifty-six years on this planet, and my life skills were decidedly sedentary in nature. I could read very quickly, complete jigsaw puzzles and crosswords with alacrity, keep baby dragons alive, and see people before Bjartur killed them.

Oh, and I was an excellent cook. But that was about it.

I'd read loads of adventure novels, but I'd never had the slightest desire to fashion my own weapons or track animals or build traps. I hadn't spent my time at home digging elaborate escape tunnels or taming wild animals to do my bidding. I had no way of contacting anyone, outside of talking to the guard posted at my gate.

That wasn't exactly true, come to think of it. I could ask Bjartur to carry a message for me. The only person who'd be willing to be approached by these venomous little flying cats we called dragons, though, would be another seer, and the only one of those I knew was Finnick. He was anything but an ally. And using Bjartur against Finnick and his dragon was not an option.

Dragons don't fight each other. They simply don't. You can't make them. If you put them into a position where they have to choose between you and another of their own kind, they'll choose dragon, every time. This put a real damper on any potential conflict between me and another seer, too. Normally Bjartur would defend me with his life. But if Finnick were attacking me, Bjartur would stand down just as Finnick's dragon would. No doubt Bjartur and Varg's grandstanding back in the woods had been a bluff aimed at Riker and the others: Finnick and I were all too aware of the limits of dragon usefulness in pitched battle.

It was even possible that both dragons would abandon Finnick and me if we dared to deliberately put them in such a position.

So using Bjartur to take a message designed to trick or betray the other seer to Finnick or his dragon was not an option. Bjartur would do almost anything for me, but not at the cost of threatening another dragon. And deceit was not something that existed between the two of us. I'd never be dishonest with Bjartur about what I asked of him. A betrayal of that magnitude, I couldn't fathom. Bjartur was the only oath I had taken in my life, and I would not break him.

I didn't know where the dragons' selective pacifism derived from. As an evolutionary survival technique, it seemed to have worked pretty well. After all, they'd survived centuries, hiding among bats and coelacanth. Their venom and zero-radius flight maneuvers made them virtually impervious to outside predators. Their only weakness lay in the care required to bring their delicate eggs through their long gestation. The bullying males of other species who posed threats to weaker specimens and infants did not exist among the dragons. So they persisted.

I wondered how different the trajectory of human history would have been if we simply refused to harm one another, like dragons did. It wasn't even possible to contemplate, really. Such humans would be so different from us as to be entirely alien. The myriad ways we damage each other is the whole of our testimony on earth.

Although, perhaps the dragons were impacting the direction of our own evolution. By submitting to bonding with us, they rendered at least a few of us incapable of much conflict with one another, however we might long for it. I would have happily ordered Bjartur to kill Finnick so that I could abscond with Allora, if I could have managed it without damaging my precious and only friend.

But I couldn't.

So at least among the executioners, combat was impossible. What an odd body of folk we were to force into unwilling peace. We could kill anyone else, but not each other. Not so unlike the dragons themselves, after all, I supposed.

At any rate, this complicated little equation meant the first solution that leapt to my mind was an impossibility. I had considered a plethora of ways I might impede the invaders' progress by slowing or misdirecting them through a message to Finnick that would allow me to sneak in and steal away Allora, but none of those would do.

Without using Bjartur as a tracker, unless they literally cut a path as they went, I'd never find them now. Subterfuge and deceit via dragons wouldn't work. And even if I could lure the whole lot of them back, I had no way of eliminating them myself. I could – maybe – figure out how to build a weapon on my own. A crossbow, maybe, or a pit full of spears I could lure them across. But I doubted my untried aim would be lucky enough to take them all out in the matter of seconds it would require, and again – I couldn't use Bjartur to lure Finnick into a hazard his dragon would be compelled to guard him against.

Perhaps all the books I'd read over the last few decades should have better prepared me for this moment, but I'd spent too much time musing over the Emily Dickinsons and the James Joyces and not enough time with the warriors and survivalists and pirates. So the only other plan that presented itself to me was decidedly unpleasant, but I couldn't conceive of an alternative.

I locked Bjartur in the bedroom with Morrigan. He wouldn't approve.

I took a few deep breaths, but other than that, it didn't do to dwell too long on what came next. I attacked myself with a vengeance, propelling myself through the next few minutes with sheer willpower and an absolute refusal to register what was actually happening.

I started with the teapot. The horrific sizzling sensation of metal on flesh was more than enough to distract me from the discomfort of slamming my ribs repeatedly against the back of a kitchen chair. I grabbed my left wrist behind my back in my right hand in a classic stretch and threw myself against the wall. Concentrating all my consciousness on the awful agony of the broken bones and burning flesh, I crunched my own skull on the cold tile of the kitchen floor. I grinned drunkenly at the smear of blood that bloomed there when I leaned back.

I wasn't even pretending when I staggered out to the guards at the front gate.

"Help," I half-whispered, half-sang as I stumbled across the flagstones.

They sprang into action like graphic novel heroes. Or at least, that was how my pain-fogged brain and blurry vision interpreted it. I surrendered to a very cautious swoon and laid down on the gravel drive, barely registering the jabs of the tiny rocks into my cheek and forehead. One of them lifted me in his arms and turned me over to face him.

"What happened?"

"They're gone," I whispered. "They're gone."

The other guard was talking on his radio or his cell phone or some sort of communication device, calling for backup. The urgency in his voice struck me funny, although actually deciphering his words required more concentration than I possessed.

It turned out I did not have impressive pain tolerance levels. Shocking.

"Who?" said the guard holding me. "Who's gone?"

"Invaders," I managed. "They – they had that child."

He almost dropped me then. I could tell he wanted to immediately take off running after them, but he decided in time that keeping me alive was his first priority. I could feel his heart pounding raucously where my face rested against his chest. Poor confused man.

"Long gone," I said, by way of easing his mind. "Last night some time. I just woke up on the floor. Bjartur – can you check on Bjartur?"

His heartrate skipped a bit faster at that. Nobody liked getting closer to a dragon.

"Hey," he yelled at his buddy. "Can you go get her dragon? See if it's still in the house?"

I couldn't see the other guard's face, but I imagined he was about as thrilled at the prospect as this one was. I knew Bjartur wouldn't hurt them, but they didn't. Even though dragons were supposed to be under the strict control of their seers, people couldn't quite shake their terror of a creature who had only to scrape their flesh to kill them instantly. The injection of a dragon's venom was a conscious act, not an automatic one, but few people understood that. I, at least, never considered it my responsibility to inform them.

As much as I enjoyed scaring the guards, though, I honestly didn't want to risk a car showing up for me and leaving Bjartur behind. The pain was beginning to overwhelm my rational thinking. I needed my dragon. "Please," I whispered. "I won't let him hurt you."

I heard the front door bang open and Bjartur came fluttering to my side. The poor fellow holding me flinched and twitched against his will like a man having a seizure as he fought to keep his position while everything in his body screamed at him to move away from the dragon. Bjartur didn't pay him the least attention. All his energy was focused on me, a mix of reproach, regret, and empathy.

Even Bjartur's disapproval couldn't counter the comfort of having him nearby. I sighed in relief as he tiptoed up onto my chest and settled himself there, his shimmering neck stretched out to tuck his head under my chin. The rumbling warmth of his body spread through me, soothing me. Gingerly the guard eased himself out from beneath me, laying me out on the drive.

"A car will be here any minute now," he told me gruffly as he stood. "They'll get you to medical attention. We'll track down these invaders once our backup arrives."

He continued interrogating me from a safer distance. "How many were there? What kind of weapons did they have?"

"Ummm..." I squinted as if I were trying to think clearly, which was increasingly true. "Three, I think. No. Four, and the little girl. A child I was supposed to execute a few days ago, but I couldn't see her and my boss took her away. The rebels thought they could use her to convince me to come with them. I think they wanted my dragon."

"And weapons?" The guard wasn't too interested in Allora, but then, he didn't know anything about her or the fact that the Justice Center had been infiltrated and their prize stolen. She'd have been just an extraneous detail to him.

"I'm not sure. They mostly used things around the house on me. But at least one of them did have a gun. They didn't want to kill me, though. They wanted me to go with them."

He was about as interested in what they wanted as he had been in Allora. I'd save those details for Fiske and anybody else at the Justice Center I had to debrief with. "Do you know which way they went?"

I shook my head and regretted it, as fresh pain speared through with the movement. "They came through the back," I whispered over the throbbing. "I was unconscious when they left, but I'd guess that's where they went back out. Besides, you'd have seen them if they came in the front."

Even from where I lay, I could see the red flush over his face. For the first time, I wondered what would be the consequence to the guards for allowing such a trespass to occur on their watch. Assuming I got away with this myself, I might well be seeing them in my execution room in a few days. A grim thought I hadn't considered.

Oh, well. It wasn't as if they *hadn't* completely failed at their job. I'd been keeping an invader child hidden in my house for days now.

That wasn't even counting Riker and her bold incursion. Then there'd been the three of us making it to the camouflage of the forest without being intercepted. All in all, they were terrible guards. Complacency and years of unsullied safety had rendered them useless. Whatever fate the Justice Center dictated for them was no doubt merited.

Still, something uncomfortable did squirm in my belly at the notion.

I closed my eyes against the thought and focused on Bjartur's heated weight. There was no chance of slipping off into a merciful faint. Authors, I decided, mostly lived lives as unexciting as their readers did. They all seemed to think that a quick smack on the skull or a strong dose of agony would render a person unconscious, but nothing could be further from the truth. It's incredibly difficult to convince the mind to slide away from pain. The opposite was true: all the energy in my entire body was focused on the burn I'd inflicted on my right forearm, so that even my breath throbbed as I sucked it in. Every heartbeat pulsed through that pain.

What in the world had I been thinking? Why a burn—incredibly painful, prone to infection, and sure to scar?

On the other hand, surely no one in their right mind would self-inflict such an injury. It had to go toward my credibility, didn't it? Fervently I hoped so.

I heard the screech of tires outside the gate, and the guard lifted me in his arms and carried me to the backseat. I bleated bleakly with agony. One broken arm and one burnt meant there was no great way to move me. Bjartur kneaded my chest and belly with his little claws in a vain attempt to comfort me. I could feel the guard arching away as best he could from the dragon who would not be moved.

"Good luck," I murmured between gritted teeth as he set me in the vehicle as carefully as possible. I kept my eyes closed, though. If my suspicions were correct, I'd be gazing all the way into his soul soon enough. No need to get maudlin over it.

I was a little anxious I hadn't been able to download my whole story concoction to the guards who were actually chasing after my erstwhile enemies, but I supposed that was the typical over-eagerness of the newly deceptive. It probably wouldn't pay to recite my account too quickly or too precisely. Perhaps the incomplete and jumbled version was the most credible.

My opportunity to elaborate came soon enough. To my surprise, the driver took me to a hospital. I'd assumed a doctor would meet us at the Justice Center. It was so very rare for me to intersect with any of the norms of society. I learned quickly it was because they wanted to do some sort of scan of my head to ensure there wasn't some unseen but serious injury to the brain itself. Luckily my own wimpiness saved me from requiring surgery for my burn, as I had snatched the teapot away before the heat could go too deep. Still, the process of cleaning it and dressing it was significantly more agonizing than I was prepared for.

My obvious distress augmented my credibility. Fiske had met me at the hospital, no doubt as much to keep me from interacting unnecessarily with anyone as to interrogate me. Certainly not out of any genuine concern. I was a commodity whose availability he had to ensure. And now, potentially, a liability he would have to dispose of.

"Tell me what happened," he said, his face tightening more with distaste than sympathy when he arrived just as the nurse was irrigating my burn. My left arm was already in a splint. Apparently it was only a sprain, not the broken bone my melodrama had insisted on. Whatever. It hurt. Although now that the good meds were kicking in, everything was feeling somewhat more endurable. "Start at the beginning. Don't leave anything out, no matter how small."

I recounted my careful tale as best I could, glad I could blame the lovely drugs coursing through my veins for my occasional stumbles and long pauses. I closed my eyes often, ostensibly on account of the pain, but mostly because I'd contracted a weird dread that Fiske might see my newfound knowledge shining in my eyes. I didn't believe everything Riker and Finnick had told me, exactly, but I also no longer believed anything I'd once thought unquestionable about my own past or my own purpose. Doubt was not a characteristic of an executioner. I couldn't afford to let it show in my expression.

Not that Fiske acted as if he doubted me. I wondered if Finnick's handlers had been taken by surprise, or if he'd been problematic for a while, a weak link from the start.

While I talked, Bjartur snoozed, curled up on my feet. The staff weren't big fans of dragons in the hospital, but there was nothing they could do about it. Where I went, Bjartur went. Fiske kept his chair pulled well up to the head of my bed, and even in my altered state, I couldn't help but be amused by how his eyes kept sliding down to where Bjartur huff-snored away.

"They said if I told you what really happened, if they were caught, they'd claim I was complicit all along. They had some idea it was better to leave me alive but silent than risk killing me and raising a hue and cry. Said they wanted someone on the inside who was already compromised. I pretended to be afraid you'd believe them, and they left me alive."

Fiske snorted at the idea I might be part of some elaborate invader plot. "Did they tell you where they were going?"

"Just that they were meeting up with some others at a secret location." That was true enough. Most of my story was true, which helped enormously, especially considering the current floaty state of my brain cells. "I don't know if it's true or not, but they claimed they had successfully recruited other executioners."

Don't ask me why I was reluctant to give up Finnick and his dragon. Maybe Bjartur was exerting some sort of emotional influence on me in my weakened state. Maybe I felt some inexplicable loyalty to him for my own part. If Finnick somehow managed to escape while the others were captured, that would be okay with me. And if he was rounded up along with the others, my vague reference to possible other rebels should cover me.

"That's not possible, is it?" I went on. "There haven't been any other executioners who've gone missing, have there?"

Fiske's eyes slid away from mine. Even after all the world-wrecking events of the past week, I was discombobulated by his obvious deception on the topic as he hastily demurred. I couldn't help wondering how widespread this wannabe revolution really was. Was the entire state rotten from the inside out, on the verge of imminent collapse, as Riker had intimated, and I was the last to know? As I certainly would be, if that ever came to pass.

Or were things precisely what they seemed to be? Riker and her ragtag band nothing more than quickly squashed cockroaches nibbling at crumbs dropped from a well-stocked pantry, the Justice Center more than capable of dealing with rare and random uprisings swiftly and effectively. It wasn't as if I was overwhelmed with executions on a regular basis. On the other hand, I had no way of knowing how many executioners there were. Or if my general pace was typical or irregular.

Basically, I was completely ignorant of everything related to my own existence.

"The Justice Center considers these invader groups very serious but small in their actual impact," Fiske assured me. "That's an absolutely classic move on their part. They're just trying to convince you that they are much more widespread and powerful than they are. And maybe trying to use a little peer pressure, too."

"One thing, Fiske." I closed my eyes again as if the drugs were starting to overwhelm me, but it was mostly because I figured it had to be easier to lie with my eyes closed. Deceit was not one of those life skills I'd ever had cause to practice, and I had zero faith in my abilities. "That child that was with them. The same one I wasn't able to see last week. Clearly Shovel was in league with them somehow. She must have given them the girl."

Fiske cleared his throat. "Shovel?"

"Oh, you know that's what I always called her. That assistant of yours I executed last week."

"Ah. Yes. Investigators are looking into exactly what happened there."

"I was thinking maybe I could take the girl home with me once they catch the rebels. Assuming she isn't scheduled for some other form of execution. She has to go somewhere, right? And Bjartur seemed to like her."

Bjartur's tail twitched, but otherwise he didn't react. It was nice to have a dragon to blame.

"Really?" Fiske's voice hit a high note of surprise. "Umm, you know a child, particularly an invader child, isn't exactly a pet, Grenda."

I shrugged, hoping I looked nothing more than mildly disappointed. "It was just a thought. I mean, if she's going to be fostered somewhere, why not with me? I already raise dragon eggs. Children can't be that much harder. Oh – and I have an octopus now, too. All sorts of maternal experience."

My voice trailed off. It was no longer necessary to fake the impact of the meds.

"I'll talk to the Center," Fiske said. "Who knows? After all, you're right. She has to go somewhere."

"Worth a try," I muttered before giving in to the darkness.

20

I woke up at home, which was more than a little disorienting. I could hear someone moving around in the kitchen. Bjartur snored softly on my feet, and the purple glow of Morrigan's tank cast a dreamy light through the otherwise darkened room.

My mouth was dry, no doubt the result of the painkillers. My arm throbbed, clear proof they'd worn off. I eased my sore body out of the bed. Bjartur raised his lids briefly and then rolled onto his back, falling instantly back asleep in a ridiculously undignified position. I hobbled out to see what was going on in the rest of the house.

The same housekeeper from the other day was pulling something out of the oven. She smiled coolly at me. "Oh, good. You're up. Mr. Fiske asked me to cook some supper for you."

"Is he still here?"

"No, he sent you home with an officer. He called me to come over in case you needed any help when you woke up."

"Ah. Well, thank you. I think I'm good now."

She nodded briskly, well-accustomed to my self-possessed ways. She washed and dried her hands and moved to the front door, collecting her handbag as she went. "Mr. Fiske said to tell you to come into the office tomorrow."

"Will do."

The house was hardly emptier after she left. I'd made it clear years ago that while I really didn't care who cleaned the house, loud personalities and space-eaters wouldn't be tolerated. So the staff they sent me now were all the reserved type.

I crossed the room and placed my palms on the humming dragon eggs, feeling their warm glow travel through my palms and up my arms, soothing and centering me. Gently I turned each one, settling them safely in the sweet-smelling straw. Outside the window, oranges and pinks streaked the sky, and I realized the sun was setting.

The aroma of hot cheese and fresh garlic finally pierced my fuzziness, and my stomach growled. The housekeeper had baked some sort of pasta dish. Perfect. Maybe a few carbs would clear these drug-induced cobwebs out of my brain. I scooped out a healthy amount and settled myself on a bar stool where I could watch the sunset as I ate.

Had Fiske bought my act? He'd seemed more focused on hiding what he knew from me than on ferreting out any deceit on my part. Then again, I'd never given him the slightest reason to doubt my trustworthiness in the decades we'd worked together. He'd known me longer than he'd known Shovel. Bedelia. Shovel. My brain flicked back and forth between the monikers. Between the identities. Hers. Mine.

People were capable of remarkable dissimulation. The past week had revealed that I was surrounded by lies, drowning in guile. Nothing about anyone I knew or even myself was true. If only some of what Riker and the others had said was accurate, then my whole existence was a hobgoblin of follies and farces. And look at me. How quickly I'd embraced deceit as a solution.

As for the people I'd executed? There was no way for me to know if they had or hadn't been worthy of their sentences. I didn't feel remorse, exactly. After all, I didn't hurt anyone. On the contrary, I saw them. I recognized and honored the soul-stuff that they were, and sometimes, maybe oftentimes, I was the first person to ever do so. Their deaths were painless and immediate. All of them, if allowed to continue, posed some sort of threat to the survival of society – whether they were a hazard politically or a drain on our resources or a danger to our safety. Whatever became of the soul-stuff housed inside those skin sacks had to be better than life here, bound up and divided and limited by mundane things like cold and hunger and sickness, time and distance.

Yet an unease pricked at me. I had always been so sure of my purpose. If my identity were a lie, how could my purpose not be?

Why tell a lie if the truth will do?

Perhaps the truth would not do. Perhaps the truth was no bolster at all to what they wanted me to become. To do in their name.

Bjartur came fluttering over to the counter. Flight was always a little wobbly over such a short distance. I retrieved some habaneros from the refrigerator and placed them on a saucer. He made happy little growling noises as he delicately tore into the bright orange flesh.

Bjartur had no qualms about our tasks, but then, why would he? Most humans were expendable to dragons. Their bonds with seers made people like Allora and me the exception. Dispatching humans required as much moral conflict for them as dispatching field mice required of a farmer. We were basically populous little vermin who mostly smelled bad and made messes but whose occasional speci-mens made fair pets. Bjartur was perfectly content to execute people as long as he could tend to little dragon eggs with me and never be asked to attack another of his own kind.

After dinner I lingered a few moments over my jigsaw puzzle of desert hoodoos, something I'd never seen and likely never would. Most nights I enjoyed traveling through my many windows of books and music and puzzles, losing myself in imaginary worlds. Tonight, though, I was tormented by the question of what was real and what was imaginary. Was there a place in the world that looked like this, all scorched sand and sheared stone and shining sun, where the footprints of civilizations thousands of years past still walked on cliff walls? Was there a reality that did not require us to take other lives to preserve our own? Could I once have been a person who began new journeys rather than ending them?

I wanted to shrug these questions off as nonsense, but my brain refused to cooperate. So I retreated to my bedroom and sat on the floor in front of Morrigan's tank. Tossing crabs into the violet water so she could pierce their shells with her little tooth and suck them out didn't do a lot for my existential angst.

Then again, Morrigan couldn't survive if she didn't eat. But Bjartur and me – we could survive without taking a life.

Or could we? Had our fates been sealed decades ago, every other road we might have taken to life barricaded and blown up by a state with motivations of its own that had nothing to do with our own personal perseveration?

It wasn't so much that our choices had been made for us. It was that we had so few choices at all. No friends. No family that we were allowed to keep. No transportation, and guards at the doors. No access to communication of any kind. Books were the only storytellers I knew. Not even a neighbor within shouting distance. Coworkers, if you could call them that, feared and despised us equally. The closest we came to human connection was the last moment we shared with the people we killed.

Suddenly I wondered if I'd ever encountered a genuine intersection before Bedelia's defection, if my entire life hadn't been one, long, unbroken road.

I'd gone my whole existence without questioning the order of things. Sure, people in books lived differently than Bjartur and I, but what made one existence more fictional than another? Some characters shat in chamber pots, some in ditches, some in toilets like mine, and some in spacesuits. Some people lived with families, some with warriors, some with nuns, some with cells and iron masks. Some women bore children and some women died in flames on a stake. Why would I have doubted the validity of my circumstances simply because they didn't match up with those I found in books? Morrigan didn't doubt her need for water simply because she saw me walking around without it.

The soreness of my body was beginning to make itself known again. I couldn't help taking a weird sort of pride in the aches. I didn't suppose it would be impressive to some gun-toting revolutionary screaming epithets into the fray, but I was uncommonly pleased with my own private rebellion. I chewed a couple of pain pills as I watched Morrigan devote herself to the painstaking task of divesting the crab of its shell.

As for Allora...who knew? I wasn't sure if Fiske was really going to make the entreaty on my behalf, or if he'd been placating me. It was possible the state wouldn't even attempt to retrieve Allora safely and would dispatch her when they captured the others. Or maybe the invaders themselves would kill Allora as the state closed in rather than allow her to be taken again.

The possibility of them all escaping was too remote to consider, in my estimation. It was true I had little enough knowledge of the world outside my gated enclosure and the confines of the Justice Center, but the state's reach felt boundless to me. Inside the cage was the only reality I could accept. The pitiful little band of idealistic scoundrels I'd met didn't stand a chance against the gleaming efficiency of the state I knew.

Tomorrow turned out to be both impossibly distant and much too near. I had little enough experience with mind-altering substances and found the painkillers deeply unpleasant. The pain itself seemed to be waiting for me, just below a surface whose viscosity was only an illusion. Actual consciousness lay deeper still, so that brief discomforts broke into my thoughts while all that was concrete and real remained elusive. When I finally shucked the night aside and readied myself for a day at the office, my thoughts were still fuzzy, my movements clumsy and awkward.

Bjartur didn't care for my muddy mind, either, I could tell. He kept sniffing around my hair and huffing quietly to himself, plainly bemused. I didn't blame him. If this was what it felt like to be drunk, I couldn't fathom how anyone ever sold a second bottle of alcohol to the same poor befuddled sot.

I plucked bleakly at a jalapeno cheese bagel in the back seat of the car as the chauffeur delivered us to the Justice Center. The bread helped settle my uneasy stomach. Bjartur shamelessly stole my peppers from his vantage point on my shoulder. I rolled down the window and let the cool wind blow the cobwebs out of my mind.

By the time we arrived, I was feeling much better and Bjartur had perked up, too. I strode in with all I could muster of my customary swagger. Should I go straight to my office or drop by Fiske's to see what had become of my request? What was the least suspicious move?

Straight to my own office would be the most typical move, and typical was good. On the other hand, I wasn't known for my patience. I honestly couldn't remember the last time a request of mine had been denied. The Grenda that Fiske knew best would march into his office and demand what she wanted, with no regard for optics. She was a creature lacking entirely in subterfuge, lies, or civility. She had no use for any such accessories.

So, knees quaking, off to Fiske's office I went, setting my face in what I hoped was supercilious expectation.

A female person who probably wasn't nondescript but whom my mind still dismissed as requiring no description sat as the gatekeeper in the anteroom, as Bedelia had done before her. I ignored the woman's ruffled noises as I sailed past and through Fiske's private door.

Fiske snapped his computer screen shut, as he always did when I came into the room, and raised his pinched face to mine with its customary expression of dread and resignation. "Grenda."

"Fiske." I bared my teeth. "Do I get the girl?"

He sighed and stood, unfolding his glasses and sliding them up his nose. I suspected it was less to improve his vision and more to put one more barrier, however insubstantial, between the two of us.

"As far as I know, they haven't even captured the invaders yet. So there's really no point in me making the request till we know more. I recommend you focus on the tasks at hand and not worry about what becomes of some random child whose mind you can't see."

I arched a brow in what I hoped was my usual disdain. "I've got little enough diversion in my days, Fiske. Allow me the occasional curiosity. But fine. I'll wait. I take it I have executions waiting for me?"

He nodded, his effort to disguise his relief at my swift acquiescence pitifully insufficient. "A passel of the newly diagnosed from the Hippocratic Institute."

"All right, then. But I expect to be updated when you hear something."

That sparked the Fiske I knew. "Obviously, I live to serve," he sneered, opening up his computer screen and sitting back down in a clear dismissal. I figured a resumption of our old and familiar hostilities had to indicate success as far as my deceits went. I breathed a little easier.

On my way out, I stopped to give my tamale and hot sauce order to the painted face propped up behind the desk. The rest of the morning passed without incident. The executions were mostly people a few years younger than I. The state had long since realized that resources were wasted on cancers and other conditions once they reached a certain advancement. All the hospital hours and medical infrastructure, the billions spent on research and pharmaceuticals, to briefly prolong a pain- and misery-filled existence really couldn't be justified. Especially for folks whose advanced disease or disability meant they'd never produce anything useful for the community again. Best to grant them a moment's peace and end their suffering.

Nonetheless, as we completed the first execution of the morning, and I summoned the guard to dispose of the remains, I experienced an unexpected rush of relief. Somewhere in the back of my mind, I'd been anxious that Bjartur might balk at our task today. That the events of the past week might have created some doubt, some reluctance, about our work. But Bjartur's mind was clear, untroubled. His swift strikes unhesitating.

I wished my thoughts were as unmuddied.

21

I almost forgot Allora in the monotony of life and death. That might sound crazy, but executions and their seeings are intense. It's no small thing to sink into a stranger's soul and then swim back out again just in time to see their living form metamorphosize into an empty husk. Desperate to refuel, Bjartur and I were eagerly tearing into our lunch and enjoying the blank silence of the bare walls when Fiske's latest assistant came heel-clacking through the door.

"Mr. Fiske will see you now," she announced. I grinned at Bjartur when she disappeared almost as soon as she'd come, her discomfort plain.

Bjartur's long violet tongue slurped the last of the hot sauce from his saucer, and he cat-walked along my arm to perch on my shoulder. I wiped my mouth and looked longingly at the two tamales still waiting. "Stay warm!" I ordered futilely and headed out the door.

Fiske was standing by his office window when we walked in. I suspected he wanted to be standing when I arrived so he could assert some dominance into our exchange, but I didn't care. A few inches of air didn't affect me the way he thought it should. I sat down and crossed my legs, allowing Bjartur to curl up in my lap and pretend he wasn't listening.

"What's the word, Fiske?"

He kept his back to me, no doubt a continued ploy at maintaining control.

"I thought you'd like to know they captured the invaders."

Bjartur's claws flexed against my ankles.

"A woman and three men were killed in the exchange. The child and a dragon escaped."

I glanced down to see a thread of blood trailing across my foot. I chose my words carefully.

"I don't imagine they'll get far."

Fiske turned to face me, crossing his arms. "No, I don't imagine so. But there's a remote chance they'll attempt to make their way back to your house. Obviously you can handle a child and a dragon, but we've posted additional staff at the gate and around the house just in case. A dragon that's been in the hands of a maverick seer for any length of time is a real hazard."

I shrugged. "Dragons possess the directional sense of an alley cat, so you might be right, but I can't imagine they'd associate my house with refuge. They were only there a few hours, and that was all nastiness and violence. I suspect the dragon will lead her to some other den of rebels."

"But you did form a connection with the child. And she may have some pull with the dragon. Of course, it's equally possible that the dragon abandoned the child once its seer was killed. This is just a precaution against an outside chance."

"Sure." I scooted Bjartur out of my lap, tucking him under my arm like a football as I stood. He hated that, and he knew I knew he hated it. I must have been near hysteria, because I had to press my twitching lips together to mask a grim amusement as he pretended to be asleep still. "I don't guess anyone will get past all that. Just remember if they do find the kid, I want her."

Something flashed in Fiske's eyes, something suspiciously like disdain. I didn't like that.

"Hey. I'm the one with the bruises and the sling here. I'm doing all the right things. You can give me this one concession."

Like my whole existence wasn't a series of concessions and accommodations.

"I told you I'd do what I can. What you're asking for is highly irregular. That just isn't how it's done."

I'd started for the door, but I turned back at those unwary words.

"Isn't how what's done?"

Fiske waved his hands, as if he were trying to physically point me in the opposite direction his words had led me.

"You know. Fostering. Placing a child with a family."

But it was too late. I thought back to what Riker and the others had told me. How seers were taken from their birth parents and placed with fosters who would carefully, deliberately manipulate and train up their empathic abilities. How those fosters would be stolen away from them in a staged trauma and the second phase of the seer's training would begin. How they'd be paired with a dragon hatchling and forever fated to live out the remainder of their lives as an executioner of the state.

How they'd exist in the same limbo as me – perfectly islanded from all humanity, alone except for one other soul who'd been similarly robbed of the society on which their whole species depended.

Bjartur's little talons clutched my shoulder tightly.

"Of course," I said bleakly, allowing him his subterfuge.

Sometimes I wish I could say the day's executions passed in a blur, but that isn't true. Whatever the cost of the sight, it was immeasurably better than the blindness in which other people apparently blundered every day.

I was the one who lived in permanent division from my fellows, but they were the ones isolated. I had Bjartur, and in the strangest way, I had them, too. Every spirit I'd seen on its way down the dirt road that carried them away from this black tarmac and into the desert of stars kept company with me still. One more reason to keep the rest of these breathers at bay. Once I reached into them, they reached into me.

That afternoon was rather tougher than usual. Each person I saw, I sank a little deeper, found it that much harder to pull myself back out. I could feel their light-spangled shadows trailing behind me, their warm hands clasped in mine long after the guards had carried their husks away. Normally I took a professional pride in how neatly I drew away all the fear from their psyche and bade them travel on with perfect contentment, but today I only knew a bleak dread that clung claw-fingered to the back of my calves.

Bjartur shared my discomfort, but his tooth was as sharp and sure as ever. Some of our kills looked so young and strong, even my will quailed, but creeping neurological disorders and fungal cancers were no mercy to endure. Better they shed these rotting skins now, before the pain and stench overtook them. They had lived well, or at least they'd had the chance to live well, and now they would die well. Surely a better end than those in less enlightened states were forced to endure—with their organs failing and their nerves consumed by agony, surrounded by the smell of their own filth and fetid blood and the disgust of those who formerly loved them.

Unbidden, the memory of Magenna and her talk of octopuses rose within me, spreading like tentacles reaching through sun-dappled water. What sort of end would I meet? I had no need of a seer to guide me on my way out. With Bjartur at my side, I had been seen, had been known, by a fellow life-traveler since I was very young, a luxury known by very few. If my brain snapped itself out of existence in the next second, my spirit would not linger for an instant. I could die whole and content at any time.

Not that I wanted to die. I quite liked living in the manner to which I'd become accustomed, though I suffered from none of the existential fears of the void that threatened so many others. Even folks who clung to one religion or another tended to seize those relics all the more tightly for the terror they'd never confess to knowing, a terror of slipping nameless and formless into a dark soup of nothingness. Faith was just another word they used to cloak their superstitions and lucky charms.

I had no need of faith. I'd seen their souls, knew as tangible truth the inescapable selves that would carry them through whatever mysteries waited out there on the other side of flesh and bone. I didn't know what we were, exactly, or where we were going, but I did know that we were real. We wore skins, they didn't wear us. And somehow I knew that we could wear whatever waited past the stars with the same ease.

So I didn't fear death. That didn't mean I was in a hurry to leave this world behind, though. I had eggs to raise and a dragon to be with. I never really suffered from the romantic longings I read about, didn't seem to have much in the way of libido. Even with all the romance novels I read, this didn't strike me as a loss. I was as deeply alive as anyone else, took at least as great a pleasure in falling leaves and blowing winds, warm cheeses and cool sheets. Maybe there was an actual genetic fluke that deprioritized those hormones for me. Maybe – if Riker and her conspiracy crew were correct – the state had taken some measures to ensure that seers were content in their single lot.

I didn't believe any of that. The truth was much simpler and more satisfying.

Bjartur was my soulmate. Caring for eggs and seeing spirits was my purpose. My life was full, my mind and heart and body fully engaged in the moments before me. How many other people, connected to one another and their societies and their purposes only by machines, could say the same? I didn't need a romantic connec-tion to feel whole. I walked in perfect contentment with my dragon. All any heart needs for survival is one other creature that truly sees them. And Bjartur has always seen me.

And I have seen him.

By the end of the day, we were equally wrecked. It wasn't like us to feel sadness over our tasks, but today an indefinable poignancy hung in the air. And we were both carefully leashing the anxiety that clawed within us, determined to give away no hint of our certainty that Allora would be returning.

Where else did she have to go? Perhaps wherever she'd first been detained, but who knew where that was? It could be hundreds of miles distant, and she certainly didn't know the way back. Not to mention she had to know nothing waited for her there. Everyone else who'd been arrested along with her had long since been executed. Most if not all of them by me.

But she'd traveled the whole distance on foot since Riker had stolen her. And unlike Fiske, I knew without question that Finnick's dragon hadn't abandoned her. Even though they weren't bonded, dragons' connections with seers were powerful. I had no way of knowing what the dragon was suffering with the loss of its partner, but I suspected the impact was devastating. It was possible the dragon was actually dying. Until it did, though, I was sure it would stay with Allora.

Loneliness is like suffocating. I feared life without Bjartur like other people feared drowning, and dragons are even more social creatures than humans are. The world is full of people who drop out of their communities, who by choice or by circumstance live solitary lives. Not so dragons. If Bjartur lost me, the one mind with whom he had a constant connection, he'd be utterly starved for air. So I knew Finnick's dragon was desperate for relief, and Allora's companionship would be too powerful a comfort for the creature to resist.

The drive home lasted a thousand years or so. When we arrived, I saw extra guards patrolling the fence. Although they'd been keeping close watch all day, one of them went into the house with us and prowled through every room, checking for intruders, before leaving us to our privacy. A uniformed stranger stood posted at both the front and back doors of the house. Fiske hadn't been exaggerating about the increased security. I couldn't help wondering how much of this was to protect me from a little girl and an orphaned dragon, and how much was to control me. The state might have mostly decided on my trustworthiness, but they were taking no chances.

Would this abate after a while, or was this my new reality? Complaining about the intrusion on my space would definitely be characteristic behavior for me, so I'd summon the requisite irascibility to talk to Fiske tomorrow, but inwardly I just wanted to sink beneath everyone's notice until all this blew over. Living on this knife-edge of tension and uncertainty was a novel and entirely unpleasant sensation for me.

Absently I chewed a painkiller and set out a dish of ghost peppers for Bjartur. We only had the one gambit, my nebulous little plan, with our new tiny perimeter. After Bjartur ate his appetizers with his usual persnickety manners, I opened the back door and released him to the open air before the guard there could even recover from his surprise.

"He needs to hunt," I said briefly. I'd never been in the habit of asking the guards around my property for permission, and it wouldn't do to start now. Better the people with guns continued to be a little cowed and fearful of the old lady with the dragon.

"Hunt?" the man echoed faintly, dismay shining in his eyes.

"For prey smaller than you," I said, baring my teeth in a smile that offered no reassurance before retreating back inside.

Bjartur would check on our little forest camp we'd constructed for Allora when I'd so naively imagined I could keep her hidden and unmolested. She might only be a child, but Allora had been a fugitive for what I figured was probably most of her life. And she had a much older and wiser companion as a guide as well. I was certain she'd head for the little refuge we'd built and hide out there. Maybe all this furor would blow over quickly, and she'd be safe there until the Justice Center gave up the search.

On the other hand, if whoever was tracking her managed to follow her trail all the way back here, I was in serious trouble. It would be an easy enough thing to establish that all the supplies out there were the same ones I'd had the housekeeper buy for me.

I didn't know at what point Allora and the dragon had become separated from the rest of the company, but I thought I'd bought her enough time to have made it back by now. It must have been sometime prior to when Finnick and Riker and the others had been apprehended. Extinguished. Perhaps the dragon, acting as scout, had warned them and they'd split up with the intention of rejoining one another after eluding capture. Or maybe Finnick had known all along. Maybe the little band had sacrificed themselves to save Allora.

I couldn't wrap my head around that possibility. Riker and Finnick both had made it clear that turncoat executioners held no exalted status among the invaders. So while the child was a valuable resource to them, I didn't think she'd command the emotional fealty necessary for immolation. Maybe they wanted to exploit the untapped abilities of seer children and adults for their own purposes, but sacrifice their lives for her? It didn't mesh. Not from a practical point of view, anyway. There had to have been some motivators, some inclinations, I'd missed.

Pondering that possibility, I scooped out some leftovers and heated them up in the oven. I wasn't in the mood to do more than that with my one good hand. I grabbed the bowl and retreated to my bedroom to eat. I didn't care for the sensation of strangers flanking my doors.

Morrigan was all but invisible behind her rocks. Octopuses knew all about sacrifice, didn't they? And yet the biological certainty of their impending starvation impeded not at all on their sense of play and exploration. I supposed in some ways that was true for all of us – death is the end of everything, after all, for everyone. But something about the deliberate exchange of their own lives for the reproduction of little beings they would never come to know seemed particularly profound.

Whether they'd fully realized it or not, Riker and her band had made a similar exchange for Allora's life. Like the octopus, they had no way of knowing if she'd be devoured by some other predators the moment she drifted away from them on the currents, if she'd learn how to hunt and how to hide. But still they'd flung themselves into the unknown as if they needed no assurance of success to justify their oblation. An innate irrationality of all rebels, I supposed. Coming to the conclusion that the will of the individual, joined to the will of other individuals, might be powerful enough to overthrow whole systems of government and economics and military establishments had to require some suspension of disbelief.

On the other hand, I knew enough of history to understand that periodically, that impossibility indeed was possible. Maybe faith in what the world labeled nonsense and fairytales was the only veritas. After all, what did fealty to the status quo bring anyone? Everybody died in the end, and however much money or power they thought they'd amassed by then, they all shat themselves when they did. Wild-eyed idealism might make as much sense as anything else. It definitely made for better poetry.

Even with the food to sop it up, the meds were making me feel fuzzy-headed. I leaned forward and tapped obnoxiously on the glass, knowing full well such irritants would only drive Morrigan farther back into her little den.

"You know it makes no sense, don't you?" I asked her.

I thought of the hours Allora had sat in front of this tank, her mind fixed in communion with the trapped ocean creature. I spent so much time walling myself up against accidental incursions of other souls, it took a serious effort of will to lower my defenses without my dragon here to punctuate the brief connection. To let Morrigan all the way in. Or rather, to ask Morrigan to let *me* in. No doubt the pills helped loosen my foundations a bit.

Peace swelled over my limbs. Rather than moving through the air, I moved with the water, the impulses of my muscles a continual reciprocity of the currents. Warmth and coolness flickered like a kaleidoscope along my nerves, millions of disparate sensations forming an infinite lens. Sand and stone and crab shell debris, color and light. Aloneness. Waiting.

Hues pulsed across my body, memories of dangers and discoveries in distant, deeper waters. I surrendered to existence, to longing. Searching.

A question intruded, not in words or thoughts, but hanging there nonetheless. This wasn't the first time Morrigan had opened her mind, her three hearts, to me. Had I learned nothing at all since then? I wasn't sure if the inquiry came from the octopus, from Magenna, or from myself.

Lost in the eye of the octopus, I might have drifted there forever, but my dragon did save me again after all. The sound of scratching intruded, discordant against the symphony of water and remembered waves.

Bjartur had lit on the little stoop of the dragon-door above the back entrance and was unlatching it with his delicate claw. The soft scrape of the door swinging open yanked me fully out of Morrigan's mind.

My eyes refocused, my thoughts oddly dissatisfied with the limited vision they now perceived. Morrigan drifted near me, her tentacles brushing the glass.

I pushed myself unsteadily to my feet, taking my bowl with me as I headed into the kitchen to see what Bjartur's reconnaissance had yielded. My dragon brother sat beside our clutch of eggs, stroking them softly with his webbed wings and humming low in his throat. His eyes were closed, but his whole body thrummed with consciousness.

"What did you find?" I asked.

He opened his eyes. Something I couldn't quite perceive pushed against our connection, like a wave of light that hadn't reached me yet. I snatched at it, but it dissipated before I could seize on it. Reassurance flooded past the fading spark. An image of Allora and Finnick's scarlet dragon curled sleeping in the makeshift shelter we'd constructed what now seemed ages ago emerged in my mind.

Finnick's dragon. I needed to stop calling the creature that. There was no Finnick now. Only Varg.

I pushed the grim thought aside. I needed to focus on what was, not what had been. Allora and Varg were safe for now. A stash of supplies at the well-hidden camp ensured Allora could stay put until the Justice Center decided the extra guards weren't needed and abandoned their hunt for the invader child, at least here. Varg would need to stay out of sight, though. A strange dragon sailing above the trees would be an immediate giveaway.

Bjartur sensed my anxiety and sent a soothing warmth my way. Varg knew the risks. He would stay under the canopy. He'd been living as an outlaw for a long time now. And Bjartur could check on them during his nightly hunts, ensure they held the course and didn't venture out until the coast was clear.

Surely the Center would soon tire of their pursuit. I understood a seer child was a resource they craved, but still. She was only a child, untrained in her skill and unlikely to survive long on her own. As long as I gave them no cause for suspicion, they should eventually decide the child had perished. I knew they'd have knocked on all the doors and alerted any populace in the area to the hazard of an invader, possibly accompanied by a maverick dragon. Even if the general citizenry was inclined to risk their own lives out of compassion for a stranger's child, which seemed unlikely enough, no one would chance the peril of a dragon's bite. Even these silly armed guards posted at my doors quailed at the sight of Bjartur, and he was fully within my control.

The house was dim already with twilight's advent. I double-checked the doors. Strangers on the other side of the walls made me uneasy in a way the guards at the gate never had. Perhaps it was my guilty conscience. I'd never been the perpetrator before, after all.

Bjartur was restless that night. Instead of sleeping across my feet as he usually did, he curled up under the sheets with me, so that the deep purring of his chest throbbed in concord with my heartbeat. But several times he woke me, fluttering away, and I knew he went to our eggs, laying his scaly cheek against their glowing shells and singing softly to them. Then back under the blankets he crawled, nuzzling his hard head against my breastbone.

22

Later the synchronicity would nag at me. But that morning at the Justice Center, I was only mildly surprised to find another witch awaiting execution. This one was a man, and I was taken aback by his age. I rarely executed an old person. The state was able to catch in its net most of those suffering from debilitating disease or disorder that might drag down society long before they aged. The same went for criminals: from what I could see, people tended to demonstrate early in life their antisocial tendencies. We eliminated them as soon as possible, before they had too much of a chance to contaminate everyone else.

Invaders, obviously, were almost always young. Venturing out across oceans and continents and armed borders required great stamina and strength. On occasion some wily old person with faded eyes and corded muscles would appear in my chambers, but it was highly uncommon.

Unlike Magenna, this witch held himself without rancor or rebelliousness. His body was relaxed, his eyes calm. He crossed the room without hesitation when the guards closed the door and he sat across from me. He stretched out a hand to Bjartur.

Bjartur nuzzled his palm, butting the bony spine of his skull against the man's wrist and purring contentedly. How interesting, to meet a man who would so cheerfully and kindly greet the agent of his own demise.

"Those guards aren't very talkative," he said to me, though his attention remained fixed on the dragon who now crawled off the table and into his lap. "I find myself feeling garrulous as I approach the Great Silence."

I could hear the capital letters, but I couldn't discern if he spoke with deliberation or humor.

"What would you like to say?" I asked.

He looked up at me then, his brow furrowed thoughtfully. "There are so many things I'd say, if they could affect change. But words that accomplish nothing are just so much more debris in a world already full of litter. I think it's less what I want to say, and more the connection I'm hoping to make. Waiting to die is a lonely thing."

I was oddly taken aback by his directness. I wasn't prone to tact myself. It was a skill best exercised by those reliant on the goodwill of others. Not only was my existence not dependent on such goodwill, I had no way of accessing it even if it existed. My guards and chauffeurs – the same people, really, with the same purpose – changed constantly, as did my housekeepers. The only people with whom I had any regular contact were Fiske and whoever manned the chair outside his office. And Fiske and I could never have been friends.

Technically, he was my boss, but I held all the power. He was incapable of hiding his terror of Bjartur and by extension, me, and I was incapable of assuaging it. Well, maybe incapable is the wrong word. Utterly unwilling is more accurate. It's hard to like people you despise. And it's hard not to despise people who fear you.

I guess I felt like Fiske should have known better. Neither Bjartur nor I were mindless killing machines. Bjartur, same as me, was a highly sensitive, perfectly trained creature who lived and operated completely at the behest of the state. Fiske knew this. But his eyes, his body language, betrayed that we were the stuff of horror to him. He more than anyone should have known better, and he didn't. I felt rather as Frankenstein's monster must have felt at Frankenstein's betrayal. So any tender feelings toward Fiske were out of the question.

I was aware, though, that people adept at social interactions employed tact as a matter of course, and that for whatever reasons, plain speaking about death rated right up there with discussing toilet adventures. Even in my line of work, encountering someone who matter-of-factly discussed what we were about to do together was very rare. The closest most people came was crying and pleading.

"Why is it lonely?" I asked, unwontedly curious.

"You have your dragon always, don't you?" he said, and I had the impression he knew far more about the realities of my everyday life than I knew about his. Were executioners common fodder among the citizenry? I wondered. Did all the people who, to me, existed only in a shadowy unreality beyond the reaches of my ken know every-thing about me? I had the sensation of being trapped in a box made of two-way mirrors.

"So you understand that human beings, like dragons, are social creatures. The first thing we experience upon coming into the world is an embrace. Everything we acquire – language, food, warmth – comes as a gift from those around us."

Not like octopuses, I thought.

"But we have to step into death alone. Even if we're surrounded by the ones we love, even if they are physically holding onto us with all the strength in their bodies, we leave them all. No matter what we believe waits or doesn't wait on the other side of that last step, no one walks out of our body with us. So a little friendly company up until that moment wouldn't come amiss."

He smiled crookedly, his hand stilling on Bjartur's head.

"The guards weren't much help for that. Probably wouldn't be good for their long-term emotional health to befriend their charges, anyway. Speaking of, I think they're more scared of you than I am. If it weren't for your dragon, I suspect your loneliness would far outpace my own. Mine, at least, is brief. But you and this little fellow here are quite nice comrades to see me off. I'd have much rather stayed longer, of course. But every adventure reaches a crossroads."

He rubbed his palms together and straightened his shoulders. It was impossible not to smile back at him – he was like a broad stone on the river's edge, drawing warmth out of the air around him simply by existing. I took his hands, met his ready gaze.

The witch was not stone at all. He was earth, sun-heated and spring-fed. Life sprawled and crept and dreamed in every granule. Here lay dead leaves, here rotting travelers who had lain down in his arms and not risen again. Here lay seeds bursting with beginnings yet unrealized. Here lay stretching roots tangling with rhizomes, nourished by magma thousands of feet below and starlight undeterred by stone and grass.

Sometimes I didn't want to look away from the souls I met. Sometimes I wanted to hold onto them, persist in their gaze instead of offering them the refuge of mine.

But I always did look away. That was my job after all.

My eyes flicked away from the witch's soul, to where Bjartur waited.

Before the witch even felt the break of our connection, Bjartur struck, and the body slumped, immediately absent its animus. I slumped, too. Bjartur hopped over to me, bopping his head comfortingly against my chest. Automatically I summoned the guard to dispose of the remains, dragged myself up to go attend to the paperwork in my office.

I'd ordered sushi from Fiske's assistant that morning. Again and again I read through the witch's file, my mind skipping through the words without absorbing them. Eventually I managed to get all the signatures in the right places. I squeezed the wasabi packets into the little porcelain dish I kept in my drawer for Bjartur. Despite my troubled languor, I laughed to see him hold the dish in his talons like a raccoon and lick the plate clean, his tongue fastidiously wicking away every last drop from his scarlet lips.

Cold rice and raw fish. I held the flavor of my own life and the lives I stole on my tongue. Strange, the remorseless mechanics of the body. Hunger and fatigue prevail regardless of the torment of the mind. Not that I was tormented, I hastened to reassure myself as I chewed and swallowed. I felt – odd, that was all. Fragmented. Divorced from myself, somehow.

We went home after that. The extra complement of guards was still present when we pulled up, and we went through the same tedious process of clearing the house as we had the day before. Once I was sure they'd lost interest in us again, I rustled up a bag of chocolate candies and tied it to Bjartur's belly with a green ribbon that obscured it from view.

There was plenty of food stashed in Allora's hidden camp, but I figured chocolate cheered everyone. I tucked a few packets of hot sauce beneath the ribbon's knots, too, for Varg. To my surprise, Bjartur seemed inclined to linger. I'd thought he'd be eager to check on his friends, but instead he wound his body around and around my arms as I readied him for his task so I had to redo the ribbon several times before I finally had him all together.

Even then, he half-flapped, half-waddled in unwieldy fashion over to our clutch instead of flying to the back door. Gently he laid his cheek against each of the glowing eggs, humming and clicking softly at them.

"Lazybones," I chided him. "It's not as if we worked a full day. Stop dilly-dallying already."

He soared over to land on my shoulder, nuzzling his spiny head against my hair. I laughed.

"You can't make me feel guilty for calling you names," I told him as we headed to the back door together. "You *are* a lazybones, and you know it."

The guard snapped to attention as I opened the door, trying to look impassive as he nonetheless shuffled well out of our way as I stepped out. Bjartur lifted away from my shoulder as soon as we were clear of the door, and the guard was too busy being brave to notice the discreet package fastened to Bjartur's belly. I watched my little dragon become nothing more than a dragonfly, a glittering streak of jeweled color arrowing through the blue sky toward the dark wood.

I like to eat sushi on occasion, but I can't say it ever fills me up for long. I have international tastes, I guess, but a thoroughly Western belly. So I rustled up some cheese dip and a bag of crunchy pretzels to tide me over till dinner.

While the cheese melted, I walked over to rest my palms on our eggs as Bjartur had rested his cheek. Thank goodness our little sojourner had suffered no ill effects from her unwilling wander. She still seemed to glow as brightly, hum as melodiously as ever. Automatically I checked their heating pad, then turned them gently in their straw. I could feel their beings lifting, straining toward me as I held the shells in my palms.

"I'm here," I whispered. "We're here. We'll take good care of you."

I carted my snacks and my books into my bedroom. Usually I liked to read in the living room, where I could watch the sunset over the trees through my back window and sit surrounded by the song of the dragon eggs. Today, though, I craved the company of the octopus.

Or maybe she craved my company.

Octopuses are awfully good at communication and play and interaction to be solitary creatures, even if biology does dictate their aloneness. The image of Allora sitting cross-legged in the violet light of the tank, her hand on the tank, as if her mind and Morrigan's were locked in silent communion, rose unbidden. I couldn't help wondering what trick of evolution made octopuses such excellent communicators and learners if they were always alone. "Thwarted destinies" was becoming a theme of my life.

I stacked up pillows and blankets to make a cozy reading and snack station down on the floor at the foot of my bed. Before I got settled, I snagged a crab and dropped it into the tank, my eyes fixed on the water near the rocks where I knew Morrigan had made her den. There was something uncommonly hypnotic and almost bewitching about the moment the octopus burst from still and invisible into sinuous, rippling strength and power. I loved that moment. When latency became impulsion, when shadow became color.

I thought about the words of the witch I had met today. Morrigan had no expectation of receiving consolation. She was a predator by nature, a huntress, a taker. Had she been in the open ocean, even the taking of a mate would have been a brief affair immediately followed by his departure and death. The only society in her existence would be the clutch of hundreds of eggs she would tend alone as she slowly starved to death herself. When they hatched, there would be no recognition, no affection, no comfort. They would propel away in a sudden burst of tiny bubbles, and she would drift at last to her unattended death.

But in this strange space, abducted as she had been, she willingly forged connections with the aliens on the other side of her confines. Gladly even, perhaps. Without language, still we spoke to one another and altered our behavior to accommodate greater interaction with each other. Morrigan, a creature bred by millions of evolutionary years to thrive in perfect solitude, made friends as soon as she had the chance. Was it harder for me? Or was I as near a friend to my curious entourage of dragons and octopus and invader children as I could be?

Between the joy of a deep dish of hot cheese and the twisting plot of the detective novel in which I buried myself, the shadows were long and deep before I looked up and stretched. It was no small feat to propel myself up from the floor with only the one good arm. I groaned as I straightened. No amount of posterior padding could prevent the achiness of an old lady sitting on the floor for hours. Old enough, anyhow.

Anxiety seized my throat as I realized I hadn't heard Bjartur coming back in his dragon door. I rushed into the living room, telling myself surely he was snuggled up and dozing with the eggs.

He wasn't.

Futilely, for no reason I could have explained, I stood on a kitchen chair and opened the dragon door, peering out into the empty expanse of the darkening twilight sky. Almost as if I thought there existed some secret channel of air only the dragon could access through that little door, along which I might yet see his emerald wings flashing back toward me. My whole being wanted to throw open the back door, to rush out into the meadow toward the woods, to scream Bjartur's name to the sky.

Quietly I closed the dragon door and slid down onto the chair, resting my head in my good hand.

Looking for my dragon was not an option.

I had no doubt where Bjartur was. Or at least, I had no doubt whom he was with.

Maybe he would still come back, I told myself desperately. Maybe he was just enjoying the company of another dragon for a while. Maybe he was keeping Allora company until she fell asleep, in case she was afraid of the dark.

Yes. That was it. That had to be it.

Regardless of what Bjartur was doing, I couldn't risk doing anything that would give him away. As far as my guards were concerned, everything had to look perfectly normal. Their purview was to remain alert to anyone approaching me or my home. I had to hope they weren't paying attention to the hunting patterns of my dragon.

It never occurred to me to doubt his safety. Even when our thoughts diverged from one another's, we lived in continual awareness of each other. I couldn't imagine that breathing would feel the same if we no longer shared the same air.

Still, when I reached out for him across the hastening night, I felt no answer. Loneliness, awful and swamping in its cold depths, swept over me. Vaguely I recognized it as the sensation that had been so devastating, so debilitating, when my parents died.

When the people pretending to be my parents left me, I suggested to myself. Every time I tried out the idea, it sounded less preposterous. The farce of my existence sounded more and more mundane.

Dully I reviewed the events of that long-ago day as they'd unfolded. In retrospect, I supposed the whole affair, from the notification to the consolation to the packing-up to the years of intense conditioning alongside my young dragon, had been precisely orchestrated. The somber-faced authorities knocking at my door and directing me to pack up just one bag. It occurred to me now, as it never had before, that there had been a unique and deliberate trauma in yanking a child who'd just lost their parents away from every possession and feeling of security they'd ever known at the same time as forcing them to abandon their beloved pets.

I hadn't thought about that in a long time. My old yellow mutt Danger and my two cats Ollie and Lima Bean. At the time, I'd been inconsolable. I couldn't believe these strange grownups expected me to leave them behind, to have them taken away by whatever agency collected or otherwise disposed of animals. Now I considered what a peculiar and particular pain that had been to inflict, solely for the purpose of soothing it later by giving me one and only one soul in the world that I could ever love again, that could love me.

Bjartur.

And now he was gone.

I could have lied to myself a few more hours, I suppose, but deceit had never been a strong point of mine. What moments before I would have sworn was entirely inconceivable I now accepted with a dry throat and dry eyes. Crying is something people do when they're sad or stunned or scared. I've seen it almost every day of my life for the past few decades. But I wasn't a person anymore. Without Bjartur, I was only a hole. A hollowness, an emptiness of everything but air and blood and pointless electrical impulses.

Absently I flexed my good hand, somehow surprised I still possessed the power to jig and jerk my marionette form with the power of a thought. I pulled open all my curtains, no longer concerned about the possible curiosity of the guards on their shifts. Somewhere out in that dark sky my dragon flew, and I wanted to look at those skies as long as I could.

Gently I gathered the dragon eggs in my arms, straw and all, and sank onto the couch with their warm, thrumming weight on my lap. I sat there all night, singing and talking to my little charges, giving my friend what time I could.

Morning came too soon.

23

My eyeballs ached as if I'd endured a sandstorm. Sunrise spilled rose-gold across the kitchen floor, cruelly beautiful. But then, everything felt cruel that morning. Mostly me. I was cruelest of all.

Carefully I laid the dragon eggs on the couch. It didn't matter now, if they spent a few minutes in the cool air. Perhaps the slight chill would slow their body responses, lull them into a merciful somnolence.

I pulled myself together. I watched myself in the mirror as I brushed my teeth, wondering if this would be the last time I tasted toothpaste. I dropped three crabs in Morrigan's tank. She, at least, could not be used or corrupted. I had a faint hope someone would place her somewhere she'd have room to explore and people to play with and food to eat, but if she were left to drift into starvation in the alone and the dark, at least she'd know how to do that. I couldn't say I knew how to do what I was about to attempt, but I was going to do my best to think like a cephalopod today.

If I stuffed Bjartur's harness with a tea towel or two and threw my cloak over my shoulders, the guards would assume that he was tucked securely against my back under the cloth when they saw me. I threw a few books and a collection of random snack foods and bottles of water into a bag. I didn't really have an expectation of getting far enough to need them, but I had to at least look like I'd had a plan of some sort.

I lingered by Morrigan's tank a while. She wasn't hiding today. Her tentacles rippled through the water as colors shifted over her skin. I wondered what they meant, if she were singing to me. Would she understand what I was about to do, if I had a way to tell her? Some choices aren't choices at all. Sometimes there is no salvation, no way out. Just a swift, merciful end.

Merciful ends are my stock in trade.

Even now, even knowing how inevitable it all was, those next few minutes stand so very dark in my memory. As if all that glorious sunlight were sucked out of the house, as if my hands moved at midnight instead of in the first flush of dawn.

I was shaking so hard I could hardly hold the icepick and the meat-tenderizer. The only consolation I could offer was song, so I sang, a tremulous, tuneless stream of promises I was breaking as I set the pick against an eggshell humming with jewel-bright color. It was awkward, as I had to stand sideways so I could hold the pick with my broken arm. I struck.

The dragon egg splintered apart. Translucent ooze slid across the coffee table where I'd set it, and a tiny, perfectly formed lavender dragon uncurled amid the shattered pieces. Almost like a flower blooming. Its tiny mouth worked piteously, its eyes rolling behind lids still sealed shut. Tiny hands, not yet clawed, gripped my fingers spasmodically.

I wasn't as hollow as I'd thought. Tears poured down my cheeks, but I ignored them, emptying all that remained of my soul and self into comforting this little one as it died in my hands. I could feel the rising terror and distress from the other two eggs as they experienced the suffering and separation of their clutch-mate. With my free thumb, I stroked the soft belly as it shuddered under my touch.

They wanted so badly to live. And they had no way to comprehend how the very spirit that had cared for and sustained them all these long months could now be the malevolence that stole all the color and music from their hours. But I was. I was their end and their only solace all at once.

It took longer than I was anticipating, longer than I was prepared to endure. But there was no turning back now. Delay would only mean prolonging the anguish of the other two, not to mention I needed to leave the house soon. So as soon as the babe sighed its last and relaxed into my palms as if in perfect trust, I laid it gently aside and picked up my implements again.

They were all the same soft twilight shade. They all clung to me and cried in tiny mewling voices as shock overtook them and their hearts stuttered to a stop. I forced myself to keep my eyes open, to hold fiercely to their connection in my mind until it snapped away. It was the least I could do for them now. I pictured diminutive octopus infants floating away from me in a stream of bubbles and kaleidoscoping colors. I wanted to sink, sink, sink down into the lightless sand of an ocean floor and surrender to the emptiness clawing out my belly, to leave the currents to the rest of the world for now.

But I couldn't. I still had work to do. Once the Justice Center realized I'd let Bjartur go, they'd know irrefutably the depths of our betrayal. Every inch of our home would be searched and maybe even razed. My pathetic and stupid effort at a hideout for Allora would be discovered. If Allora and Varg and Bjartur were to have any chance of escape, I had to lead the state away from them, if only briefly.

I'd come to understand why Allora had come back, even if I didn't accept it. She had decided that Bjartur and Morrigan and I represented some sort of safety, some familiarity she craved, even in the face of everything I'd done to dissuade her from that point of view. Varg, undoubtedly, was accompanying her in fulfillment of Finnick's last wish. Although Varg and Allora had fled the invader company before Finnick and the others had been killed, Varg would have known the moment his lifelong companion died. The dragon would be suffering its own trauma even while it attempted to execute its duty to its friend. I couldn't help feeling a surreal and unjust kinship with the scarlet dragon.

I couldn't know, of course, but I suspected what Finnick had intended was for Varg to guide the child to some other enclave of these rebels, some cohorts who would keep her safe. It would only have been Allora's stubbornness that brought them back into my reach. Now that Bjartur had joined her, they would follow Varg's lead again and make their way to a life I couldn't imagine, to a place I couldn't betray, even under duress.

I didn't know Varg at all, but I knew Bjartur. He'd done the inconceivable, but now that I'd faced facts, I could see his intentions clearly. It wasn't Allora he'd chosen, though he'd formed an undeniable bond with her. Bjartur had chosen his own kind, and in that, he'd chosen himself, for the first time since I'd met him as a hatchling.

Dragons were among the canniest of creatures, humans included. Bjartur hadn't spent the last three-plus decades in the halls of the Justice Center without understanding exactly what the consequences would be of the choice he'd made. I had no doubt he'd have pushed Allora and Varg to begin their trek yesterday evening as soon as he'd reached them. Wherever they'd gone, they at least had the benefit of those hours. I had to believe that. And the fact that Varg had managed to bring Allora back to her little camp here without the Justice Center's goons tracking them told me the other dragon had the necessary subversive skills to keep my friend as safe as any invader or rebel could ever be.

I didn't think my particular direction would have any relevance. As soon as they captured me, they'd realize I was nothing more than a diversionary tactic. All I needed to do was move, move as far and as swiftly as I could, until my movement was stopped.

It didn't make any sense, but I couldn't bear to leave my little dragon babies exposed to the cold air and the gazes of the guards who would soon be ransacking the house. I covered their still forms with a quilt and piled the straw from their manger over the top of it, as if I could yet offer them warmth. The tears had dried on my face, and my cheeks were stiff with salt.

I pulled on my galoshes, adjusted my cloak over the dummy dragon on my back, and headed out the kitchen door. The guard posted there looked surprised, but I didn't really know why. Guards had hardly been standing duty at my doors long enough to have an idea of my usual habits.

"The car will be coming for you in about an hour," he told me.

I shrugged as if disinterested. "We'll be back well before then," I lied baldly.

I struck out in the opposite direction of the wood where I'd built Allora's sanctuary. The sun shone harshly in my eyes. I squinted, watching dewy fog dissipate from wildflower fields in its glare. Prisming droplets of color and light floated like octopus babies rising in a current that would carry them far, far away from their birthplace.

24

Walking was a surprising struggle. My whole body ached. Besides the self-inflicted injuries still nagging at me, I hadn't slept all night. My joints jangled and jumbled under too-tight skin. I'd never been the hiking type to begin with, and years of soft and sedentary living had hardly prepared me for trekking of any distance. My head pounded.

I trudged on across the open meadow, conscious of the guard's eyes on my back. I did my best to amble and pause now and then as if I were admiring the sunrise or watching the course of the bumblebees, even as my heart knocked furiously in my chest. I told myself I would pick up the pace once I got into the camouflage of the trees, but I wasn't sure I'd be able to go much faster. I felt thirty years older than I was.

The morning's chill still lingered in the shade of the wood. Soon enough, I knew, the sun would churn that damp cool into sticky heat that clung to the skin and clogged the lungs. I didn't take the clearest route – I bushwhacked my way through the undergrowth and left heavy footprints in the mud.

I felt no remorse, no regret for the little charges I had cared for so tenderly all these months only to rob them of their flight so shortly before they would have hatched. When you have no choice, remorse is a fool's indulgence. I couldn't care for them myself. I wouldn't allow them to share Bjartur's fate, divorced from one another's company and utilized only to kill. To leave them to die alone would have been a coward's choice. So I'd done what I had to do, for their sakes. Accepting and acknowledging that was the least I owed them.

Guilt is a decision we carry, but grief is the destiny of all life. The eagle father mourns when the horned owl steals his eaglet. The elephant tribe pauses to remember their dead every time they pass the mud pit. The rose bush grows thornier year by year. I walked with the image of my dead lavender children fresh before my eyes, with the sensation of their soft, silken skin under my thumbs. My every breath came too easy, as theirs had come so hard.

I tried not to think of Bjartur. Our paths would not cross again, I knew. I had to trust that whatever lay before his little band, he would go on. He would find a way. Perhaps he and Varg would find other dragons, build a lair, become a tribe again unsullied by human interference. Perhaps the three of them – Varg, Bjartur, and Allora – would craft a fugitive life of their own. Perhaps they would join their strength to some impossible and nonsensical endeavor of the invaders and rebels.

It didn't matter now. Not to me. To know what became of my friend was not given to me. And I didn't want it to be. I was too much of a fatalist to put much hope in possibilities. As long as I knew nothing, all things could be true. Bjartur could be free. Allora could grow up to be an old lady. Morrigan could be released to the sea.

Unwillingly, I thought of Bjartur as he had been yesterday afternoon, his leather wings draped so gently over the clutch, his cheek bent to their jeweled thrumming shells. He would hate me, hate me consummately, if he knew what I'd done. He might kill me himself if he were to encounter me.

But he had to have known I would do exactly what I'd done. He had done the unimaginable, after all – he'd broken our bond and chosen someone else, some *dragon* else. But there was no question of me ever doing the same. I would choose Bjartur. Always. And the only way I could choose him was to abandon them.

I should have sensed something when I'd watched his tender farewell. Should have picked up on the glimmer of his intentions when he left me. Perhaps that hurt as deeply as anything. Bjartur had withdrawn from me, so deliberately, so gently, I hadn't even recognized what was happening. That last spark I hadn't been able to seize...desperately I wished I could have held onto it. Could have had some goodbye to cling to when my end came.

Would he be haunted, I wondered, by the ghosts of the little dragons he'd left to their deaths? Would there one day be other eggs, other infants, he would help to protect and perhaps even to raise? I was glad, at least, he had not been there to see what my eyes had looked on. Grateful he'd done what I could never do and broken our psychic bond so that he would not need to carry those awful moments forward with him, on every current, in every dawn.

I didn't bother trying to navigate the forest. My goal wasn't to get anywhere, after all. I had no interest in escaping the state, if that were even a thing I considered possible. I wasn't a witch, capable of summoning life and sustenance and even medicine from the earth. I wasn't a rebel or an invader with a romantic cause and a thirst for violence. I wasn't a person who could connect with others, build relationships and form bonds and survive through some weird inter-dependent network of give and take.

I was a bird who'd lived her whole life in a cage, and I had no interest in the wide sky with its storms. I had a friend out there who needed a few hours, and securing those for him was my only purpose. Beyond that, nothing mattered.

The body doesn't heed the travails of the spirit. It gets hungry, gets tired, gets full of waste, regardless of all else. I ate, I drank, I rested, I emptied myself. I went on.

The whole affair took much longer than I thought it would. I didn't know why. Perhaps they were slow to realize my defection was deliberate. Once they'd found the dead hatchlings, they'd have had to know. At any rate, it was almost a day and a half before the dogs treed me. I say, treed, because I absolutely climbed a tree when I heard them approaching. Death doesn't trouble me, but dog bites do.

I don't even know why they set the dogs on me. It wasn't as if I hadn't left a trail as clear as day in the mud and through the underbrush. Maybe snarling dogs made little men feel more like the savages they dreamed of being. As if they really were stewards and masters of all living things, instead of just eaters and devourers and ravagers.

I waited patiently, legs swinging from a low branch, for the soldiers to catch up to their beasts. It wasn't as if I were trying to get away, so there was no point in climbing farther up when I was just going to have to climb down again. I couldn't help smiling to see how excited and pleased with themselves the canines were. I thought of my dear old dog Danger for the second time in three days after not thinking of him for decades.

Did these dogs hold as near a bond with their people as dragons did with their seers? Could such a closeness exist between any two creatures, and we simply missed it most of the time? I didn't know. And it was too late for me to find out now. It was too late for everything.

I ate the last of my chocolate and hard cheese while I waited. I savored every morsel on my tongue. I focused on the press of the bark against my thighs. I stroked the soft, veiny leaves that made my brief bower. I strained my ears over the baying of the hounds to cling to the trills and whistles of the birds as they fluttered about their tasks, untroubled by our small drama. Their little nests would still make safe haven for unbroken eggs, regardless of what became of me. I reveled in the heat of the sunlight where it fell through the branches and rested on my shoulders. I raised my face and felt a soft wandering breeze against my cheeks.

. . .

Things have been unpleasant since then. It's difficult for them to believe I'm no master-conspirator. If I had known anything at all of the rebels' plans, I'd absolutely have given them up. My pain tolerance is low, and my endurance lower still. I suffer no illusions about my stalwart character. I never intended to play hero, only to create a brief stopgap in the hours, a stopgap through which I prayed Bjartur had escaped.

They underestimate how well they really did brainwash me. I'm not a rebel. Not a revolutionary. I didn't want to change the world. I didn't even want to change my own world.

I did want, briefly, to share some kindness with a child whose whole existence was a mystery to me. That aborted kindness somehow led to all this distress and disaster. Love, however poor and paltry and fevered, is perilous to all systems.

I think they've finally accepted I have no information to offer them. I'm glad. The ordeal is almost over now. I understand what that last witch was telling me. It is very lonely, waiting to die. He had me in the end, and Bjartur, to come alongside till he made it over the bridge. But as a seer, I will have no such mercy. Just as I could not execute Allora, no seer will execute me.

It's useless, but my mind keeps reaching out, out, out, for my dragon. I don't know how not to look for him. But he has learned not to look for me. I am trying to be thankful that is so.

I wonder how it works for people like me. The state's not monstrous, after all. In fact, the Justice Center prides itself on its consummate humanity. My meals always arrive like clockwork. Some nondescript person who says not a word shows up after every interrogation session with fresh bandages and ointments, though I can't help but wonder if half-healing is part of the torture. They give me fresh linens and clothes when I soak through mine with blood and sweat. Even this water I drink is crisp and cold.

A firing squad, maybe. I've read about those. But it seems

contrary to the state's general purposes to have so many people involved in the machinery of death. They generally prefer to protect their populace from the ugly side of security and success. An injection, maybe. A hanging. Maybe some sort of wild animals, so that no person is involved in the act itself at all.

Now I'm just horrifying myself to no purpose. My brain insists on playing through the possibilities, as if it can somehow prepare for what comes and face it with some aplomb. Considered dispassionately, I imagine they'll choose something simple and eminently practical. Something cheap and easy. There is no pageantry of expiry in our society.

And the state has no fear of my spirit remaining in this place. Unlike the people I executed, I was seen clearly almost all my life. I had Bjartur, and Bjartur had me, a gift so rare it left no room for even a single regret. I am alone now, but all my life, I have had a true friend. It is no hardship to leave this broken body behind. I have been loved.

Bubbles rise at the edge of my vision, and I think I see tiny octopuses moving toward me, their many-colored tentacles rippling with light like the songs that used to play over the dragon shells in our clutch. For a moment, I am disoriented, almost frightened, but then the truth claps through my thoughts like lightning – the glass of water.

Of course. So simple. No need to even waste a needle.

I watch the baby octopuses as the cell seems to fill with water. I gasp, but only once – breathing undersea is surprisingly simple, after all. As the current carries me up, up, toward the narrow tunnel of light where my window used to be, I see Morrigan's great eyes resting on me. I do, I think muddily. I do understand something about octopuses. I do.

I look for a glittering green dragon, search anxiously for flashing wings above the water. It isn't quiet here in the depths, not at all. All sorts of songs rise around me, echoing calls and deep-throated pulses of consciousness. But what I long most to hear, the tuneless music, the rumbling purrs, of my friend, I cannot find.

In the undulations of sound, I make out a single word: Ana. Whether it comes from within me or without me, I cannot tell.

I wash out in a strange tide.

<u>The End</u>

ACKNOWLEDGMENTS

Just as every book becomes a thousand books in the hands of a thousand readers, each book begins as the contribution of a thousand dreams, most of which are impossible to singly identify. My undying gratitude belongs to Elizabeth Gilliland, who first believed in this strangest of strange little books, and who devoted countless hours and much spirit to its success. Many thanks to all the scientists, explorers, and aquariums around the world who uploaded and streamed their encounters with cephalopods to share them with the rest of us. The joy, delight, and wonder these creatures bring to the earth and its oceans cannot be overestimated. The community of writers and readers on Twitter who believe in me and encourage me and most importantly, befriend me, is a haven in a world that too often breaks our hearts. And as always, my deepest thanks goes to my husband, my patron, and my best friend.

ABOUT THE AUTHOR

Cassondra Windwalker is the multi-genre author of several novels and award-winning poetry collections. She has lived in the South, the Midwest, and the West, and presently writes full-time from the grim coasts of the Frozen North. Regrettably, she has no dragon of her own, but she keeps company with corvids, anemones, moose, and mycelium. Readers are invited to reach out to her on Twitter @WindwalkerWrite.

ALSO BY CASSONDRA WINDWALKER

Fiction

Bury The Lead

Preacher Sam

Idle Hands

Hold My Place

Poetry

The Almost-Children

tide tables and tea with god

BAYOU WOLF PRESS

Bayou Wolf Press is an independent publisher of quality fiction. If you enjoyed this book and would like to support us, the best thing you can do is leave a review on Amazon, Goodreads, or wherever you review books. If you'd like to learn more about our press, sign up for our newsletter, and stay informed on upcoming books, please visit our website.

www.bayouwolfpress.com

www.ingramcontent.com/pod-product-compliance
Lightning Source LLC
Chambersburg PA
CBHW061210210726

48294CB00006B/1806